# CLAWS

# CLAWS

## MIKE AND RACHEL GRINTI

 SCHOLASTIC INC. / NEW YORK

First published in the United Kingdom in 2012
by Chicken House, 2 Palmer Street, Frome, Somerset BA11 1DS.
*www.doublecluck.com*

Library of Congress Cataloging-in-Publication Data

Grinti, Mike and Rachel.
Claws / Mike and Rachel Grinti. — 1st American ed.
p. cm.
Summary: Twelve-year-old Emma Vu, having just moved into a trailer
park inhabited by magical beings known collectively as crags, begins
learning cat magic in hopes of finding her missing sister, Helena.
ISBN 978-0-545-43313-6
[1. Magic — Fiction. 2. Cats — Fiction. 3. Missing persons — Fiction.
4. Fairies — Fiction. 5. Sisters — Fiction.] I. Grinti, Rachel. II. Title.

PZ7.G8872Cl 2012
[Fic] — dc23

2011048362

10 9 8 7 6 5 4 3 2 1     12 13 14 15 16

Printed in the U.S.A.   23
First American edition, September 2012

The text type was set in Adobe Garamond Pro.
The display type was set in Windlass.

Interior book design by Kristina Iulo

TO JOE MONTI,
FOR BELIEVING IN CAT MAGIC

CRAG FACT OF THE DAY:

*"The word* crag *was first used as slang to refer to trolls because of their gray, rocky, 'craggy' skin. Today, it's popularly used to refer to any magical creature such as dwarves, ratters, hags—and cats."*

CragWiki.org

# CHAPTER I

"Is that it?" Emma asked as they pulled up in front of a rusty gray trailer. The yard was overgrown with weeds and surrounded by a rotting wooden fence. Behind the trailer, a line of oak trees marked the boundary of the magical forest.

"That's it," her dad said. "That's our new home."

Emma's stomach dropped. She couldn't think of anything to say. Their old house hadn't been big, but it was near her friends, and there'd been a library and park Emma could walk to. She missed it already. The trailers here all looked beat-up, the roads were full of potholes, and the only thing she could walk to was the forest. The trees grew close together, and between them were huge bramble bushes and weeds as tall as Emma's waist. Years ago, before Emma was born, the forest had magically grown and swallowed up half the city, but now it just sat there, still and menacing.

It was all her sister Helena's fault. They wouldn't have had to move if Helena hadn't disappeared three months ago. But Emma tried not to think about her. She was tired of crying. It never made anything better. It didn't bring her sister back. And she tried not to think about what her friends would say when they found out she was living in a trailer park with a bunch of crags. She'd tried to explain it to her parents, but they didn't listen. Some days it felt like they forgot she was still there.

"Does it even have running water?" she asked. "We're not going to have to put out buckets when it rains, are we?"

"It's got water and electricity and everything," her dad said. "It won't be so bad, I promise."

Her dad had also promised the police would find Helena. Then he'd promised that the private investigators he'd hired would find her. He hadn't kept either one of those promises. Emma knew it wasn't his fault, but still. You were supposed to keep your promises.

"It's only temporary," her mom insisted. "Just until we get our finances together and your dad takes care of a few things."

2

"Think of it as an adventure," her dad added. "The police told me it's safe enough for humans as long as we stay out of the forest."

"As long as we stay out of the backyard, you mean."

"Nope, just you," her dad said. "We're still allowed in the yard." He glanced back at her from the passenger seat, smiling.

It wasn't a very convincing smile. Emma knew he was trying to act like everything was okay. But every day that Helena didn't come home, his face looked thinner and more of his hair turned gray.

"What kinds of crags live here anyway? Are there trolls and stuff?" She'd read about trolls on CragWiki, but she'd never seen one in real life. They mostly stayed in the forest these days, like a lot of crags that were too strange or dangerous to fit in with humans. But not too dangerous to live in Emma's new backyard.

There hadn't been any crags at all in their old neighborhood. She'd only ever seen any when they went into the city or drove past the forest, and then only through the car window. Meeting a troll or a harpy sounded a lot more exciting when you were reading about one on CragWiki than when you might have one as your next-door neighbor.

She looked past the trailer, trying to see into the shadows of the forest, but she didn't even know how to tell if a troll was lurking. From the pictures she'd seen, trolls were huge and had rocky skin with plants growing all over. Maybe they just blended into the trees until it was too late . . .

"Your father says it's just dwarves and some satyrs and dryads," her mom said.

"Mostly just dwarves," he said, though something about the way he said it made Emma wonder what he wasn't telling them. "That's not weird, right?"

"Uh-huh. Maybe if we were dwarves," Emma said. But it made her feel a little better. Dwarves, satyrs, and dryads were supposed to be pretty safe.

They got out of the car and her mom popped the trunk. They all grabbed a box and walked up the metal steps to the trailer's front door.

"So you weren't scared off after all," someone called from the neighboring trailer.

Emma looked over to see a man sitting in a hot tub. Well, the top half of him was a man. She was pretty sure the bottom half was all snake. The end of his scaly tail hung over the side of the hot tub. The way the scales glistened grossed Emma out, and she couldn't help shuddering even though she knew it was rude. She tried to focus on his face instead.

"I saw you moving boxes earlier, and I thought: That human can't possibly be moving in here. But here you are, with a family and everything." The way he said it was almost a question. Like he found it just as odd to have a human neighbor as they did living with crags.

"Yes, here we are," Emma's dad said, trying to sound friendly. "I'm Chien Vu. This is my wife, Hanh, and my daughter Emma."

"George. George Simbi," the snake-man said.

"Well, it's nice to meet you, George," her dad said. There was an awkward pause. "You're a naga, yes? I used to see your, ah, your people back when I was a kid in Vietnam. I've never met one, though."

"And you still haven't," Mr. Simbi said, just a little frostily. "The naga, though similar in appearance, originated in Asia. The coatl, which is what *I* am, were native to what you think of as Central America, and a few parts of South America." He sounded like one of Emma's teachers.

"Oh," Emma's dad said. "I didn't know that."

"Please don't mind him, George," Emma's mom added quickly. "He tends to put his foot in his mouth sometimes. I think he likes the taste. I'm sure we'll all get along just fine, though."

"Oh, it's all right, I suppose." Mr. Simbi sighed. "Humans never seem to be bothered to learn about us. Not that you can really blame them. Most crags you'll meet here are respectable citizens like me, but there are some in these partsssss . . ." He trailed off, hissing the last part of the word, and stared past them to the trailer on their other side.

Emma followed his gaze. She thought she could see something peering out from between closed blinds — a pair of eyes and wrinkled skin — but then she blinked and it was gone.

Her mom put a hand on her dad's arm. "Chien, what does he mean by that?" she asked in a low voice.

"Nothing, nothing, just . . . you know how it is, the forest nearby and all that," her dad said. Mr. Simbi looked like he was about to say something, but her dad went on quickly. "It was nice meeting you. I'm sure we'll talk more later. Come on, Ems, I want to put this stuff down before my arms fall off."

He opened the door for Emma and her mom, then propped it open with the box he'd been carrying. Emma wondered about the eyes next door as she walked in. They'd looked like human eyes, she thought. But then again, Mr. Simbi's eyes looked human, too, if that's all you saw of him.

Inside, the trailer had a heavy, musty smell. The carpet was torn and stained, and black specks of mold dotted the edges of the ceiling. The curtains were old, the bottoms in tatters. Her parents had already moved in most of the stuff from their old house, and boxes were piled up all over the living room. It felt cramped.

Emma set the box she'd carried in on top of the nearest stack. "This isn't so bad, I guess," she said, even though it was pretty bad. "Once you guys clean it up."

"Once *we* clean it up," her mom corrected.

Maybe it really wouldn't be as terrible as she thought. Maybe it really would be an adventure. Their old house had been almost too big and too quiet without Helena. She might have been loud and obnoxious sometimes, but she had filled the space with fun and clothes and magazines and interesting bits of junk.

"Do you want the grand tour?" her dad asked. He waved a hand at the kitchen. It was separated from the living room by a wooden counter. "Here's the kitchen. Not exactly professional, but it'll do. Go through it and you'll find your bedroom on the right, then the bathroom, then our bedroom at the end."

Emma headed toward the narrow hallway past the kitchen, then stopped. Some of the boxes in the kitchen had been torn open, and huge piles of cereal flakes were strewn across the tiled floor.

"Mom! You didn't tell me this place had mice."

Her mom hurried to look, and her eyes widened as she took in the mess. She leaned down and ran her finger over a wide slash across the top of one box. Claw marks. "That looks too big for mice . . . I hope we don't have to call an exterminator, we really can't afford—"

"Is it ratters?" Emma asked. "I bet it is. Big, giant ones from the forest."

"I'm sure it's not ratters," her mom said uncertainly. "We don't have any secrets they'd be interested in. Certainly not in our cereal. It's probably just a raccoon and I'm sure we've scared it away by now. Why don't you start moving things into your room while I clean up, okay?"

"I still think it could be ratters," Emma mumbled as she went back for the box she'd brought in, and carried it down the hall.

As she got near the door of her new bedroom, though, she heard a scrabbling sound that made her freeze. She heard it again, a faint scraping of . . . claws on metal?

"Um, hello?" she whispered at the door. "Is someone in here?"

Emma braced the box against the door frame and put her hand on the doorknob. Her heart was pounding. She wasn't actually sure she *wanted* to see whatever it was. But it was in her bedroom, and she couldn't stay outside the door forever.

She took a breath and turned the knob. The door swung open, and at the same time a metal vent cover in the corner of the room fell back into place. Emma dropped the box and ran over to the vent. She sat on the floor and peered through the slits, hoping to see something, but it was too dark.

"And don't come back!" she called through the vent, feeling shaky and ridiculous.

A sound that could only be laughter echoed back at her, then all she could hear was her own breath. She sat, stock-still, for several moments. Obviously it wasn't just a raccoon. Raccoons don't laugh at you. And it was probably too small to be a ratter.

Ratters were the size of a short human, according to CragWiki, though Emma had never seen one. They stayed in the forest since no one liked having them around. Not just because they were huge rats that could talk, either. Everyone said ratters could find things out about you, things nobody was supposed to know.

But at the moment that seemed less scary than whatever was hiding underneath their house. Who knew what creatures lived in the forest? Things CragWiki didn't even know about, things that might come crawling back at night while she slept . . .

She pulled the box over the vent. What if it wasn't heavy enough? She'd need something heavier. More boxes, maybe some duct tape.

The room was barely six feet across. The hardwood floor was stained and scratched, and the window frame was warped and yellow with grime. She wrinkled her nose. It smelled like some kind of animal had been living here. Clumps of dirty white fur had collected in the corners.

"Emma, what are you doing in there?" her mom called. "Didn't I just tell you to start carrying things into your room?"

Emma edged out of the bedroom, keeping an eye on the box to make sure nothing was trying to move it, and walked back through the kitchen into the living room. "I want to get my stuff out of the car first," she said, though really she just wanted to get out of the trailer *right now*.

"Just as long as you're carrying something somewhere useful," her mom said. She was still trying to clean up the mess in the kitchen. "And don't go wandering off, all right?"

"I think I can manage to walk to the car and back without getting lost," Emma said.

Her mom looked up at her. "I'm serious, Emma. Don't go off on your own, don't go near the forest, don't talk to anyone you don't know. You mustn't be rude, but try to be smart, okay? If something doesn't feel right, come right home."

"Okay. I'll be careful," Emma said. Her mom hadn't been this paranoid about letting Emma go somewhere alone since Helena first disappeared. It was broad daylight outside, and Mr. Simbi seemed more likely to lecture Emma to death than to hurt her somehow.

She went outside, staring at her feet as she walked down the steps of the trailer to their car.

"What're you doing here?" a voice croaked to Emma's right. Emma jumped and spun around, nearly tripping on the last step. A hunched old woman stood in the other neighboring yard, staring at Emma and gumming her lips. "They said human childrens don't come to crag places."

The eyes were the same ones she'd seen peeking out of the neighboring trailer. And there was something strange about this old woman. Her small, wrinkled face looked somehow familiar, even though Emma was sure she'd never seen her before. Her eyes were bright and clear.

"I'm not a child. I'm twelve," Emma said.

The old woman sniffed at the air. "Still a child, still a child," she sang softly.

There was a gentle breeze, and Emma smelled cinnamon and baking cookies. "Are you baking something?" she asked. She leaned forward, inhaling the delicious smell.

The old woman laughed. "Can't be helped, can't be helped. We both smell food, but we'll both go hungry."

Then the smell changed. Instead of cookies Emma smelled Vietnamese pudding—coconut and banana and ginger. Her mouth watered and her heart ached. She loved that smell. It was her only memory of her grandfather, who had died when she was a little girl. The old woman seemed so kind and sweet. Emma wondered if she could go inside her trailer and have some of the pudding.

She found herself taking a step forward.

"You stay away from her, hag!" Mr. Simbi shouted from his hot tub.

Emma reeled away until her back was against the car. "You're a hag?"

"Snakes." The old woman spat on the ground. "Snakes is always hissing, always slimy, always underfoot." According to

CragWiki, the only way to recognize a hag was to look for double rows of sharklike teeth hidden behind their gums. Emma now realized that if you were that close, it was probably already too late.

Emma noticed now that the hag wore a long, shapeless brown dress stained with dirt, and a gray shawl wrapped around her head. She wasn't wearing any shoes, and her yellow toenails were long and curled. She no longer looked kind or sweet.

"You should stay away from her, especially at night," Mr. Simbi said. "The government took her teeth so now they say she can't eat children anymore, and she's allowed to live here for free. But you can't trust hags. I bet she couldn't resist cooking someone's child even if she couldn't eat them afterward."

"Yes, yes, listen to snake-man's hissing," the old woman said. "Very dangerous is hags, can't be trusted." She sniffed the air again and smacked her lips, then dug around in the pockets of her shapeless dress and pulled out two cotton balls and a small bottle of clear liquid. She unscrewed the bottle's plastic cap, and the smell of alcohol and mint made Emma's nose twitch. Then, grumbling to herself, the hag soaked the cotton balls in the liquid and stuffed one up each nostril.

Emma slid along the car toward the front door of her own trailer. Her mouth felt dry and her heart was beating quickly. She imagined herself going inside the hag's trailer and never coming out. The sweet smell of dessert faded as Emma began wondering exactly how hags cooked children.

"You're scared now, yes?" the hag said in a slightly nasal voice, her eyes watering. She grinned her toothless grin and took a step forward. "Now you'll change your mind, move away. Won't have to smell you anymore, won't have to feel so hungry."

"Ha! You think they'd be here if they had any other choice?" Mr. Simbi said. "Why should they care about your hunger anyway? No, you're stuck with them now!"

"I'm not scared," Emma said, but her voice shook. "Not if you don't have any teeth." She could run at any second. The trailer, her parents, they were right there.

The hag scowled at her.

"It's not like I want to live here, either," Emma said, and suddenly the words came pouring out of her, as if the hag really was her kindly old grandmother. "My dad wanted to move here because he thought maybe the crags would help him if he was one of them. Like they could help him find Helena. That's my sister. She ran away from home and the police couldn't find her, so my parents hired private detectives. Only they couldn't find her, either, and then my dad lost his restaurant. We don't have any money for anything, and my mom says it's cheaper here and—"

"How old was she?" the hag asked.

"What? Sixteen. Almost seventeen."

"Mmm, no, didn't eat her," the hag said. Her words sounded comforting, even though they shouldn't have been. "Never liked hunting ones that old. Not scared enough when they get lost. Hard to smell. But there was one, all scared and alone . . . so long ago, but I still remember how his bones crunched, and the marrow . . . oh yes, so sweet. It was a ratter child, with so many little crunchy bones." She sucked on her gums. "They're a lot like human childrens, once you're past the fur and the squeakings."

A shiver ran up Emma's spine and she felt sick. She clutched her stomach and took several deep breaths. She might have read about hags on CragWiki, but hearing it from a real hag, hearing the way she said it, that was a lot worse. "What, um . . . what do you eat now that you don't have any teeth?"

The hag made a disgusted face. "Cans. With meats in them. Tastes like chalks and gives me gases and bellyaches, but I never, ever, ever feels full." She sighed and rubbed her stomach. "But at least no one hunts me. Hard for old hags, with ratters and howlers in the forest, humans everywhere else. So I eat cans, and I live in peace, until today."

"Don't you feel bad for her!" Mr. Simbi called out. "I never understood how you humans can treat honest, hardworking people like me so badly, but let monsters like her have a free place to live."

"Never did like snakes much," the hag said, louder than before.

"Their eggs is disgusting inside, and the little ones is like eating worms."

"Like you could ever get near a coatl egg-room. Back when my people ruled the Aztec empire, we hunted your kind for sport until every last one was dead and burned!"

"Emma, what is going on out here?" her mom said, walking down the metal steps. "What've you been saying to Mr. Simbi to get him so—" She stopped abruptly when she saw the hag. "Oh! I'm sorry, I didn't see you there. Do you live in the other trailer? I thought there weren't any other humans living here."

"She's not a human. She's a hag," Emma said. "But her teeth are gone, so I don't think . . ."

Her mom gripped the handrail so tight that her knuckles turned white. "I see. Emma, get inside, now."

"But—" Emma started to protest, even though she wanted nothing more than to run away from the hag.

"Now!" Her mom turned back toward the trailer. "Chien! Get out here!"

Emma could hear her dad's footsteps thudding through the kitchen, then clanging as he ran out onto the steps. "What? What happened?"

"*That*," Emma's mom said, pointing toward the hag. "That happened. Would you mind explaining what that . . . that *thing* is doing living next to our daughter?"

The hag nodded and hobbled toward Emma's parents. "Not safe, not safe for human child. You will have to move away, yes, must keep child safe from horrible monsters."

"Hanh, calm down," her dad said, holding up his hands. "The police said she's completely harmless, and she mostly stays inside during the day anyway. I was going to tell you, but I only found out two days ago, with the house practically sold already, and—"

"Don't you dare tell me to calm down!" her mom shouted, and then she switched to Vietnamese to continue yelling. It was almost always bad when they switched to Vietnamese.

This was supposed to be her life now, Emma realized. She wanted to get away—from Mr. Simbi, from the hag, from her parents yelling most of all—but where could she go? Down the road? Into the forest?

For once, she did what her mom said and went back inside. Not that it was much better inside the trailer, with her smelly room and the thing inside her vent, laughing at her. Her mom was busy worrying about the toothless old hag, when something else was living right under the trailer. They'd be lucky to survive the night.

There was nowhere to sit in the living room, so she sat down on one of the boxes. What would Helena have done? She always seemed to have an answer for everything. Emma thought about what things used to be like, what *normal* used to be like. Her old house, her old room. Her sister.

Helena probably would have said something sarcastic, like she didn't care that their parents were fighting or that they'd lost the house. Then she'd have lounged around, reading her glitter-covered faerie magazines and gushing over the descriptions and illustrations of their fancy clothes and expensive parties.

Emma always thought Helena was just pretending that she didn't care when she acted like that, but maybe she really hadn't cared at all. Otherwise, why would she run away, and not tell Emma anything? Why didn't she call or leave a message on Emma's HangOut wall or something?

She wished Helena would come back. Then everything would be right again. Then she wouldn't feel so alone.

CRAG FACT OF THE DAY:
"*The average child between two and fourteen years old
is one thousand times more likely to be hit by a car
than to be eaten by a hag.*"
CragWiki.org

# CHAPTER 2

"You know, it wasn't very polite to block up the vent like that."

Emma sprang up from the box she was sitting on and looked around, trying to figure out where the voice was coming from. Then she saw the thin, ragged-looking cat lounging on the window-sill, half hidden by the curtains. His fur was patchy and so dirty Emma couldn't tell what color it was supposed to be. One of his eyes was missing and there was a pink, sunken scar in its place.

Emma only knew a little about cats, but what she knew wasn't exactly comforting. They could talk, but they rarely bothered to talk to humans. They could change their size and become huge, the size of lions or bigger. And they'd been known to hunt humans, though there hadn't been any incidents in a long time. That anyone knew about.

"You were in my room before, weren't you? You laughed at me," Emma said. She backed away and looked around for something to defend herself with. "What do you want?"

The cat's voice was deep and lazy, almost bored. "I'm glad you've finally figured out that I'm not a ratter. Perhaps next you'll use those same claw-sharp wits to realize I can't open doors very easily, and you've blocked up my way in and out. I'd rather not have to fight to get back into my own home."

"You own this trailer?" Emma asked doubtfully.

"Of course I don't *own* it," the cat said. "What would be the point of that? I live here, so it's my home. At least, for now."

"But it's our home now. We're moving in today." Emma hated the way it sounded, but there it was, the truth. Her parents weren't suddenly going to yell "Surprise!" and reveal this was all a big joke.

"Obviously you're moving in," he said. "But I was here first, so you're going to have to learn to share."

"I'm not allowed to have pets," Emma said automatically.

The cat's one eye narrowed dangerously. Emma paled. A cat wasn't like a dog or a gerbil. Saying a cat could be a pet was almost like saying Emma's parents kept *her* as a pet. He was just so much smaller than most other crags, even if he could talk. She back-pedaled quickly.

"I mean, um, my mom wouldn't want a cat living with us. I don't think she likes crags very much." She hesitated. "Is it all right to call you a crag? Is that an insult?"

"You can just call me Jack," the cat said. "Anyway, I'm sure she'll like *me*. Everyone does, sooner or later. I'm quite charming."

Emma eyed his dirty fur. "Are you sure you aren't thinking of some other cat? Like one with both eyes who still remembers how to clean himself?"

Jack laughed. It was a strange sound. Not quite a purr, not quite a human laugh. "You caught me at a bad time, that's all. A couple of other cats have been playing a little game with me. It's called 'Hunt Jack, Then Kill Him.' I'm afraid I haven't had the chance to compose myself just yet."

Emma's eyes widened. "Kill you? Not for real, though, right?"

"Oh, I'm pretty sure it's for real. I took something of theirs. Doubtless my charm will win them over and they'll calm down. But until they do, I need somewhere to hide, and this trailer works quite well."

Emma wasn't sure whether to trust anything the cat said—for all she knew, he was friends with the hag and the snake-man. "Couldn't you just turn yourself into something so they couldn't find you? Cats do that, don't they?"

"Other cats do, sometimes. Unfortunately, these days, I'm

without a pride. No pride, no magic. My attempts to correct this have unfortunately only caused me further trouble. It's a sad state of affairs." He eyed Emma and began to tear lazily at the curtains with one claw. "Though I think an opportunity might present itself soon enough."

"So, um, where are these killer cats now? They're not around here somewhere, are they?"

"Still looking for me in the forest. If they were nearby, you'd know about it."

"Oh. That's good, I guess." Emma sat back down on the box. "I'm sorry you lost your pride and your magic and stuff. I lost someone, too. My sister, Helena."

"Oh, please. What good is a sister? We're talking about cat magic, the most powerful magic in the world, and you're talking about someone who was in the same litter as you. You can always get more sisters."

Emma stared at him. "You . . . you can't just say things like that. You can't . . . what if she's been kidnapped? What if something horrible happened to her?"

"Then she should get herself unkidnapped. I don't see why you're worrying about it." He yawned. "Now, it's a pretty big inconvenience for me having to share my house with you—"

"You do realize my parents are moving in, too, don't you?" Emma cut in.

"—but I might be able to make allowances if you share your

food with me. I remember trying something from a little metal box once. It opened at the top, and the smell . . ." He licked his whiskers.

"You mean it was in a tin can? Like tuna or something?"

"Bring me some and we'll see," Jack said.

Emma sighed. "All right, but my parents can't know you're here, okay? You're going to have to hide in my room." She eyed his dirty fur. "And you have to clean yourself up if you want to sit on my bed." Letting him stay might not be the best idea, but if he really didn't have any magic, it was probably safe enough. Safer than being outside with the hag anyway.

She realized then that it was quiet outside. Her parents had stopped arguing. Jack's ears pricked up as footsteps sounded on the metal steps outside the front door. "Hide! Quick!" Emma hissed, but Jack was already on his feet and bolting for her bedroom.

The door opened and her parents walked in.

"Who were you talking to?" her mom asked.

"No one," Emma said. "I was looking for one of my schoolbooks but I couldn't find it."

"Well, you'd better make sure you do. We can't afford to pay the replacement fee if it's lost." Her mom sighed. "I'm going to drive you to school so you don't have to walk, and you're going to have to stay inside, especially after dark."

"I thought the hag couldn't do anything. If it's so dangerous here, why—"

"She can't," her dad said. "Your mom just wants to be extra careful, that's all."

"What about Mr. Simbi? Could he hurt me?"

"Mr. Simbi is safe enough, just a little stuffy," her mom said. "He seems like a nice enough man. Snake. Coatl. Just . . . try not to bother him, that's all."

"But don't ignore him if he talks to you," her dad added. "We don't want him to think we have something against crags. All right?"

"So . . . I'm not allowed to go outside or walk to school, but it's perfectly safe, and we don't want the giant snake-man to think we have anything against crags. Is it all right if the hag thinks we have something against crags?"

Her dad clapped his hands together. "How about we get things straightened up, then I'll make us a nice dinner? Emma, what would you like?"

Emma hesitated. She knew he was changing the subject, but it had been a long time since he'd asked that question. "I dunno . . . maybe garlic lasagna?" It was one of her favorites, even better than phở, which was Helena's favorite.

"Hmm. I think I can manage that. It's been a while since we had Italian night, hasn't it?"

For a week after Helena had disappeared, Emma's dad had cooked phở every night—just like their grandmother used to make it. As though it would bring Helena home somehow. After that, when there was still no sign of Helena, he'd tried to keep cooking, but everything seemed to go wrong. Like he didn't really care anymore. That's why he'd had to sell the restaurant and they'd run out of money.

Emma's mom smiled. She'd always joked that she married a chef because she liked to eat but didn't like to cook. "I think that sounds very nice. We'll put the table together and move the rest of the furniture, and then you can go to the store. I'll make you a list of some other things we need."

Emma could almost smell the rich garlic scent wafting up from a pot of cream sauce, could hear it bubbling gently. Her stomach rumbled. She'd missed her dad's cooking. She hadn't even realized how much she'd missed it. Home wasn't really home without it. Or without Helena. Emma's sister would be horrified by their trailer, though. Her room back home had been completely color-coordinated, like it was a photo from a magazine, and it smelled of her cucumber body spray instead of mold and cat.

"Can you get me some tuna?" she said, remembering her promise to Jack.

"Since when do you like tuna?" her dad asked, his brow furrowing.

Emma shrugged. "Since I had some at Marie's house." She'd have to tell them about Jack soon, but not just yet.

The next hour was spent dragging furniture around the cramped rooms and stacking boxes in corners until they could be unpacked.

Her parents were in the middle of trying to move a dresser when there was a knock on the door.

"I'll get it," her dad said.

Emma followed him, weaving between boxes. There was another knock just as her dad opened the door. On the other side stood a short man in a wrinkled suit and sunglasses. He was barely Emma's height, but a lot heavier, with a huge belly and thick arms that strained the seams of his sleeves.

It was a dwarf, Emma realized.

"I'm looking for Mr. Vu," the dwarf said. "You him?"

"Yes, that's me," her dad said. "Is there something I can help you with, Mr. . . . ?"

"Heard you were asking around. For information. That you might be looking to talk to certain people about certain business."

"Yes, that's right," he said. The hope in his voice was obvious, and painful to hear. "I'm looking for my daughter. I was hoping someone might be able to—"

"Payment first. Gold if you've got it. Or gemstones."

Her dad nodded and stepped aside to let the dwarf in.

"Hanh?" he called. "We have a visitor. Where's that bracelet we were talking about the other day?"

Emma's mom stopped just outside the living room, her gaze landing on the dwarf. Her shoulders slumped. "Oh. Of course. I'll be right back with it."

They waited in awkward silence for a few minutes. Then Emma's mom reappeared, a thin gold-and-silver bracelet in her palm. The dwarf fumbled with his sunglasses, stuffing them carelessly into a pocket, then held out his hand. It shook slightly.

"This was my grandmother's," Emma's mom said quietly as she set the bracelet in the dwarf's calloused palm.

His eyes widened as he ran his fingers roughly over the links. "This is old," he whispered. "Dwarven-made. Don't recognize the marks, though." As Emma watched, his eyes changed from a dark gray to a bright, shining gold.

Then he closed his fist over the bracelet and jammed it into another pocket, rubbing his eyes until they were dark gray again. "I can take you to meet some . . . contacts, but you'll have to go into the forest. I'm not promising your safety. Okay?"

"Okay," her dad said.

"Then get a move on already," the dwarf said. "Because I'm not getting any younger." He turned and stomped down the metal steps.

Emma's dad glanced back at her mom and smiled his serious smile. "I'll be back, don't worry. Maybe I can make us dinner some other night." Then he gave Emma a quick hug and whispered, "I'm not giving up on Helena. We're going to get her back. I promise." He followed the dwarf out of the trailer.

Emma and her mom worked in silence for the rest of the evening, and dinner was cheap Chinese takeout, the sort her dad always used to complain just gave food a bad reputation. Of course, lately he ate whatever he was given without comment of any kind, like he couldn't taste it anyway. Jack, at least, seemed quite content with the pieces of chicken she snuck away from the table.

It was late by the time her dad finally came home. Emma was in bed, listening to her MP3 player, Jack curled up beside her. His one eye was closed but she could tell he was awake. She threw a blanket over him so her parents wouldn't see him. Jack growled, and scratched her leg as she stood up.

Emma opened the door to her room and peeked out. Her father's face was drawn and gray. He looked exhausted and his clothes were dirty.

"Who did you speak to?" she asked. "What happened?"

"Nothing," he said absently. "I need to talk to your mother. Go back to bed."

He went into the master bedroom at the back of the trailer. A few moments later, she heard the murmur of her parents' voices through the walls, but couldn't make out what they were saying. She didn't want to know. Obviously whatever her dad had thought he could do in the forest hadn't worked out, and that meant they were going to be stuck here for who knew how long. Until she got eaten by one of the neighbors? Maybe then they'd care.

"I wish *I* could just not care," Emma said as she sat down on the bed.

Jack opened his eye. "Then don't."

"Maybe you just don't care because everyone wants to kill you." Emma sighed.

"Caring about things is a trap," Jack said. His tail swished angrily. "If you care too much, you can't ever really be free because you won't give up the thing you care about."

Emma was too tired to think about this.

"What am I supposed to do? I can't just stop caring about my family. And I don't want to."

"If this sister of yours cared about you, she wouldn't have left, you know. What has caring for her gotten you?" He was quiet for a moment, then sidled up to her and leaned against her arm. "I like it here. But it's not going to be any fun if you're so miserable all the time." He began to purr. "So maybe I can help you find her. That's what human friends do, right? Help each other? Like you helped me by letting me stay here and bringing me something to eat."

"Help me find her how?" Emma said cautiously.

"Cat magic."

"I thought you said—"

"Not mine. Yours."

"What?" Emma laughed, but Jack just blinked at her. He was being serious, she realized. "But I'm not a cat. How can I have cat magic?"

"It's been known to happen. Not very often, but there are cat stories about humans with cat magic. You just have to trust me." He wiggled his backside for a moment as if he was about to pounce on something, then settled down. "This plan solves both our problems. You get cat magic; the pride stops hunting me. Then we can do whatever you want. We can find your sister and bring her back. Or you can turn her into a mouse. Or just forget about her. But we wouldn't have to hide in this trailer. We could go anywhere. Do anything. You wouldn't have to be scared anymore."

"But . . ." Emma didn't know what to say. She swallowed, trying to ignore the fluttery feeling in her stomach. The feeling that maybe she could fix things. Was this how her dad felt every time he came up with some new plan to find Helena? But he was her dad, she thought. He was supposed to take care of things. She was just a kid.

Everything was happening too quickly. A day ago she'd never even talked to a crag before, and now here was a cat telling her she could have magic. And magic wasn't just talking cats and Mr. Simbi. It was hags and dwarves and a forest full of things that even CragWiki didn't talk about.

"Cat magic isn't for scared little mice," Jack said offhandedly. He looked her up and down. "I don't think you look like a mouse, though."

Emma knew her parents would want her to say no. But what would they do if they had the chance to save Helena? She took a deep breath. "Would it turn me into a cat?"

"It might. Would that be so bad? It's the best thing to be, otherwise cats would just turn themselves into something better."

Emma frowned. "If I turned into a cat, or grew fur all over, or anything like that, it'd be harder to find Helena."

"You'll be able to turn yourself into whatever you want once you master the magic," Jack said. "How long that takes depends on you."

Emma met his one-eyed gaze, but it was impossible to know what he was thinking. She wasn't sure what to make of him yet, or of half the things he said. But here he was, offering to help her get the one thing she wanted most. Maybe her parents wouldn't even have to know, so if she failed, if she couldn't find Helena, they'd be no worse off. At least she'd be doing something, instead of hoping Helena would come home before they had to eat ketchup for dinner.

If there was a chance, she had to take it.

Even if it meant she might turn into a cat.

Being a cat would be worth it, wouldn't it, if she brought her sister back?

*I'm not scared*, Emma told herself. *I'm not a mouse.*

But her stomach felt like a lead ball, and her head was light and dizzy. She had to try three times before she could get the words out.

"All right," she said. "I'll do it."

"I know." Jack yawned and stretched, tearing holes in her sheets with his claws. "I could tell you would make a good cat. Your future pride is still hunting for me, so I won't be able to get the Heart's Blood until morning when they're asleep."

"The what blood?" Emma said.

"You'll see," Jack purred. "But they're going to be pretty angry with us."

*"Despite protests from parents,* Gnomebots *remains one of the most popular after-school television shows for its positive portrayal of magic."*
CragWiki.org

# CHAPTER 3

Emma squeezed her eyes tight as the door to her room swung open, flooding the room with dingy light from the hallway. She heard the creak of a footstep, and her mom's voice. "Emma, I have to go into work early, so I need you to — *what is that?*"

Her mom's screech startled Emma awake. She sat bolt upright. "What? What is it?" She automatically checked the walls of her room, expecting to see a giant centipede or a spider. Then she saw that her mom was pointing at Jack. She started breathing again. "You were supposed to hide," she told the cat.

"Why? It's just your mom," Jack said. He closed his eye and put his head back down.

"Emma." Her mom grabbed her arm and pulled her out of bed, dragging her to the doorway. "Do you know this creature?"

"Um. Kind of," Emma said. "He was living in the trailer before we moved in, and I didn't want to just kick him out. His name is Jack."

Emma's mom pinched the bridge of her nose between her fingers, grimacing. These days she mostly just looked tired and sad, but for a moment Emma was reminded of the way her mom used to look every time Helena came home late, or sneaked out of the house, or bought another outfit their mom hated. It looked so normal.

"What were you thinking? You can't just let a strange creature stay in your room. How did he get in here? After yesterday, I can't believe you'd do something so irresponsible!"

"He can talk," Emma interrupted. "That makes him a person, not a creature."

Her mom pointed at the door. "He has to go, right now."

"But he doesn't have anywhere to go," Emma said. "He doesn't even have any magic, so he's completely harmless. What does it matter if a cat lives with us anyway? It's not like we aren't already surrounded by crags. At least he doesn't want to eat me, *unlike* our new neighbor."

Her mom was going to ruin everything. If she kicked Jack out, he might not want to give her cat magic. What if he left and didn't come back at all?

For a moment Emma thought of telling her parents what Jack was offering. But they wouldn't understand. They'd say she shouldn't get involved, that it was too dangerous. Her dad might even try to make Jack give *him* cat magic instead. But they wouldn't care about Jack. Her mom was ready to throw him out without even listening.

"I'm sorry if you don't have anywhere to live," Emma's mom said to Jack, "but this is our home now, so you're just going to have to find somewhere else."

Jack jumped down from the bed and gazed up at her. He looked small standing by her feet like that. "You humans never think," he said calmly. "You should be glad it was me Emma found in her room and not something that might have harmed her. How do you expect her to stay safe if you don't have the slightest idea what you're keeping her safe from?" His tail lashed from side to side. "But *I* know. And I can help. So think on that before you leave me to fend for myself without food or a home or magic."

Emma's mom turned on him, her neck a blotchy red. "You think we can't protect our own daughter? Is that it? Well, I can protect her from *you*, that's for sure. I want you out, do you understand? Or I'll call the police, or animal control, or whatever it takes to get you out of here!"

"But, Mom—"

"Emma, get ready for school. You have ten minutes."

"I'll go for now," Jack said. "But you might want to be more careful so this kitten doesn't disappear, too. Human children go missing all the time. There's worse things in the forest than cats, you know." He bared his sharp teeth in what Emma thought was a grin, then bounded past her mom and vanished down the hall.

Emma's mom stared after him, her mouth open like she wanted to yell at him but had no idea what to yell. Her hands were clenched into fists so tight they shook.

"He doesn't mean it," Emma said. Though she couldn't help feeling he had a point.

"Emma, I don't want to see that creature on our property again, do you understand? And if you see him somewhere, don't talk to him. I don't trust cats, with or without magic."

"Can we talk about it later?"

Her mom sighed. "Later he'll be gone. He's not your friend, Emma."

But Emma didn't believe her. Jack had already been a friend to her. No one else had done anything to help. *He'll be back,* Emma thought.

As soon as her mom went to make sure Jack had actually left the trailer, Emma cleared her things away from the vent and left her bedroom door ajar for him. She found her school backpack, then she pulled a wrinkled T-shirt and jeans from her bag of clothes and got dressed.

Her mom was waiting impatiently by the door in her crisp blue scrubs, stethoscope hanging around her neck. "Come on," she said. "I can't be late to work again."

The air outside was cool, but bright orange sunlight filtered through the trees, promising a warm day, hinting of summer, of vacation and sleepovers at her best friend Marie's house, and not getting out of bed until *Gnomebots* came on. Only summer wasn't going to be that way this year.

Emma's mom got into the car and reached over to open the passenger door from the inside. The handle on the outside didn't work anymore.

As they wove through the trailer park, Emma saw more crags leaving for school and work. A beat-up old station wagon drove past their trailer, a dwarf behind the wheel. His long beard was slung back over his shoulder, and a sticker on his bumper read "My Other Car Is a Mine Cart." A satyr boy ran down the road, backpack swinging wildly. His feet made a quick *clop clop clop* sound. Behind him walked a very thin girl with green skin and long fingers. Emma thought she must be a dryad. There were even a couple of ratters, running quickly on all fours, their long pink tails trailing on the ground behind them.

Everyone knew that there was a crag school around here somewhere, near the forest. It had been a human school once, until the magical forest took over Old Downtown. Emma wondered what they learned there. Probably cool stuff, like magic.

Then her mom pulled out of the trailer park, and the forest disappeared behind the privacy walls of the nearby shops and houses. Years ago, when her parents were still kids in Vietnam, Old Downtown's narrow cobbled streets and colonial townhouses had been the center of the city. But then something happened—no one was really sure what, though humans thought there was some kind of twisted magic involved and blamed the crags, any crags—and a forest had started to grow. Emma's history class had spent most of the fall learning about it.

In only a week, trees that looked like they were a hundred years old covered most of the city. Humans had moved out of Old Downtown, leaving their broken homes behind them. Most of the crags had stayed, living in the forest or in trailer parks and houses around the forest's edge.

Since then, a New Downtown with wide roads and glittering skyscrapers had been built, and modern treeless suburbs on the other side of New Downtown had become home to those humans who could afford to move. Though a few crags worked in New

Downtown, the only ones that lived there were the faeries. Of course, no one really thought of them as crags.

Fifteen minutes later, her mom pulled into the drop-off lot in front of Emma's school.

It felt too weird. Like things were still normal, when they weren't at all. "I'll try to be back at three o'clock to pick you up," her mom said.

It was early—earlier than Emma had ever gotten to school when she used to walk. There were hardly any kids lining up outside. Marie was there, though. She was always panicking about being late for classes, even though she was so smart Emma knew none of the teachers would have cared.

"Hey," Marie said, but she didn't quite look at Emma, and her voice was quiet. Distant. She'd been acting weird ever since Helena had disappeared, like she didn't know what to say around Emma anymore.

"Did you watch the latest episode of *Gnomebots*? I didn't get to see it because of the move, and we don't even have Internet yet."

"My dad said I'm not supposed to hang out with you anymore," Marie said slowly, still not meeting Emma's gaze. "I wouldn't care what he said, you know I wouldn't, but it's just . . ." She shrugged. "He threatened to take away my cell *and* my laptop. You know how he is about . . . crags." She said it as if Emma was a crag herself and might be offended by the word.

Emma stared at her friend. "What does any of that have to do with me?"

Marie shrugged again. "You know. You live with them. He thinks you might be a bad influence, that I could get hurt."

"So, what, because I had to move, I'm suddenly not good enough to be your friend?"

"No! I don't think that, Emma." And a look came into her eyes—a pitying, supposedly sympathetic look Emma was getting to know well. The look that said, *I'm sorry you lost your sister, but it makes me sad to be around you, and can't you just get over it already so I don't have to feel that way?* "We can still hang out at school, okay?"

"Okay," Emma said dully. "See you inside, then. Wouldn't want you to be seen talking to me." She turned away and headed for the back of the line, not looking to see if Marie followed.

She wasn't exactly surprised. Well, not about Marie's dad. When he was a kid, his home had been destroyed when the magical forest had overtaken Old Downtown. He was always going on about it.

The bell finally rang, and the line of kids started filing through the doors. The line inched forward because of the magic detectors the school had installed at the beginning of the year. They were supposed to stop kids from bringing dangerous magical items to school, but it just made getting into the building take so long that they were usually late for homeroom.

When she went through the magic detector, someone started making loud beeping noises, and everyone laughed. At least Marie had tried to be nice about it. Then again, Marie was probably the one who told Casey and Amanda where Emma was moving to, and they probably told everyone else, so this was kind of Marie's fault.

*I don't need stupid friends like her anyway.* She hoped Marie's laptop got a virus and blew up.

A boy named Matt jogged to catch up with her. "So what it's like living with all those crags?"

"What do you care?" she asked, eyeing him suspiciously.

"I just thought maybe you could help us with the crag problem we're having, since you're an expert and everything. See, these crags are sneaky. They look just like girls, but actually they're ugly trolls that stink like swamp, and the—" He stopped suddenly and sniffed. "Wait . . . you're not . . . It's you! You're the crag!"

Matt and his friends were always picking on one kid or another. People always laughed, mostly because they didn't want to be the ones getting picked on. At least, that's what her dad had said. It didn't make it any better. Emma couldn't think of anything to say that wouldn't just make things worse. She tried to walk faster, but he followed her.

"So have you tried showering? Maybe that would help with the smell. I'm only trying to be helpful." He stopped in front of her, blocking her way. "What about your little friend? Is she a crag, too?"

Emma noticed Marie at the same time Matt did.

"There's one of them now," he said. "So what kind of crag are you? You don't look like a troll. A ratter, maybe?"

"I'm not a crag!" Marie said quickly. "I hate crags."

"Then why are you friends with one, ratface?" he smirked.

"I'm not! She just . . . she just follows me around all the time and tries to copy my homework. Nobody likes her. I mean, she smells, right?"

*So much for still being friends at school,* Emma thought. While Matt laughed, she ducked past him and ran to homeroom. She didn't see Marie again until third period. Their desks were next to each other, but Emma refused to look at her ex-friend.

Marie set a note on Emma's desk. Sorry, the note said. Gnomebots was awesome. I DVR'd it. Want me to burn you a copy?

Emma pretended she didn't see it. When the bell rang, she stood, knocking the note to the floor, and walked away.

*"During the Salem Cat Trials of 1912, six men and thirteen women were accused of being cats that had changed their shape to look like humans. All were hanged, though they were proved innocent after all of them failed to turn into cats upon their death."*

CragWiki.org

# CHAPTER 4

Emma didn't pay any attention in any of her classes. All she wanted to do was get home and see if Jack had come back yet. If everyone was going to think she was a crag, she might as well hurry up and become one already. What was that thing he was going to get? A Heart's Blood, or something?

Her mom was late. Emma wasn't sure if she was happy to wait or not. On the one hand, it gave her more time to brood. On the other, at least no one was around to make fun of her. But after sitting on the curb for half an hour, the scale was definitely tipping to *not* happy.

When her mom finally pulled up, all she said was, "Sorry about that. I have to go back to work, but your father's home. Come on, hurry up."

"I might as well have changed schools," Emma said, sliding into the passenger seat. The vent rattled softly as it blew cold, dry air over her arms. "Marie's dad won't even let her talk to me." Not that she wanted to talk to Marie anymore, but still.

"That's ridiculous," her mom said, frowning. "As soon as we get the phone hooked up I'll give him a call, I'm sure he'll—"

"No! You can't do that. Just leave it alone, okay? I don't care anyway."

Her mom took her eyes off the road for a moment, looking at Emma with a worried expression. "You want to tell me what happened?"

"Why can't Jack stay with us?" Emma demanded. "And don't say because he's a cat or a crag, because those are the only friends I'm going to have."

"Emma, this isn't up for debate," her mom said. "It's all right to be friends with crags. With some crags. But you have to be careful. They're not like us. Even if they look almost human, they're just . . . they're different. Dangerous."

"I thought different makes you special," Emma said sarcastically. "Remember? When that kid was making fun of me in first grade, you were all," she mimicked her mom's voice, "'*You're special, be proud of your heritage, it's good to be different*.' What happened to that?"

"I'm sorry you're having a rough time," her mom said. Her voice had dropped to a whisper. "But we're doing this for your sister. It's probably the only chance we have left."

"Yeah. I know," Emma said. She wiped at her eyes.

They drove the rest of the way in silence. Her mom stopped by the trailer just long enough to let Emma out, then drove away again. Emma trudged up the metal steps to the front door and threw it open. "Dad?" she called. But he wasn't in the living room watching TV, or in the kitchen. She was just about to knock on her parents' bedroom door when the door to her own room creaked open behind her.

"He's gone to the forest again," said a familiar voice. "Trying to talk to more crags. Fool."

"Jack!" Emma ran to her bedroom and closed the door.

Jack jumped onto the bed and faced her, his eye half closed in a sly, satisfied expression. She noticed he'd tracked leaves and dirt all over her blankets. He lifted his paw.

Below it lay what looked like a small, soft marble, glowing with a dark red light that seemed to pulse.

She peered at it. "Is that what you were talking about? The Blood thing? It looks like a hair ball." She'd meant it to be a joke, but her voice didn't rise above a whisper. The more she stared at it, the deeper the color became, drawing her in. She could see something in it now, dark swirls, like shadows dancing in the firelight.

"Well, that's rather insulting," Jack said. "This is the Heart's Blood of a pride of cats. It's the source of their magic. Whoever has it becomes the leader of the pride. Its heart. That's you. You're going to be the Pride-Heart."

With some effort, Emma pulled her eyes away from the Heart's Blood. "I don't remember reading about anything like this on CragWiki. Cats can turn into things, right? Like bigger cats and stuff? Is that what I'll be able to do?"

"It does a lot more than that. Enough magic for you to get your sister back. Now pay attention. You'll have to learn to rule over the rest of your pride. You'll need them to help you track down your sister."

"But I don't want to rule over anyone," Emma said. "It doesn't seem right."

"There's more to it than that. Because a Pride-Heart is the source of a pride's magic, they want to be ruled. And every cat wants magic. You still want to find your sister, don't you?"

"But couldn't we try to find my sister together, just you and me?"

"The pride'll still show up sooner or later, expecting magic. Better to give it to them, right? Anyway, we still wouldn't be as effective as lots of cats looking for your sister, would we?"

"No. I guess not," Emma said. "But if this thing's so important, how'd you get it?"

Jack spent a moment cleaning his face. "All you need to know is that the last Pride-Heart is dead. There's a vacancy and . . . the Heart's Blood doesn't respond well to cats like me. Anyway, the Pride-Heart is nearly always a female. This way we both get what we need, so it's all for the best, isn't it?"

"You killed the Pride-Heart?" Emma said quietly. She tried to picture Jack hurting something. It wasn't a nice thought.

"Maybe a little," Jack said dismissively. "But that was before I even met you, so there's no point in worrying about it now."

Emma swallowed and glanced at the Heart's Blood again. As soon as she looked at it, her gaze seemed to sink into it again. Or was it that everything around it started to seem less real somehow? She didn't have to wonder why it was called the Heart's Blood. The red light, the way it pulsed steadily. Even the way Jack described it, with magic flowing from the Pride-Heart to the other cats . . . Blood, the life of the pride, pulsing through them from the Pride-Heart.

But what if it was too late? What if Helena was already . . .

"Is it dangerous?" she asked, trying to forget what she'd been thinking.

Jack just looked at her. If he'd had eyebrows, they would have been raised.

"Mom and Dad would kill me if they found out I was messing with magic like this," Emma said. She was stalling, she knew, but she couldn't help it. "And Mom already doesn't like you."

"Trust me," Jack said.

Emma's heart pounded. She hesitated for a moment, then reached down and picked up the Heart's Blood. It felt soft and fuzzy, like a peach, and it smelled like a forest after it had rained: heavy and wild and full of darkness. She hadn't even known darkness could have a smell until that moment. "What do I do with it?"

"I've only seen a cat become Pride-Heart once. She lapped it up like it was water. You could try that. I don't really think it matters how you do it, though. Tell it what you want, and it'll know what to do." His ears flicked up. "But you'd better make it quick. Your pride's close. They'll be here any moment now. They're drawn to the Heart's Blood."

Emma focused on the small marble. It seemed to purr in her hand and the shadow-shapes within it had started to look like cats. They were searching for something. Searching for *her*.

"You won't get another chance," Jack hissed, and there was hunger in his voice now. "What's that word you humans are always throwing around like it means something? Love? Don't you love your sister? Don't you want to save her? Do it!"

"She's my sister. Of course I love her," Emma said softly. Then, almost without knowing what she was doing, she brought the Heart's Blood up to her mouth. She tasted the deep, wild darkness on the tip of her tongue. She smelled it as it filled her nose. Heard it like the hiss of a great cat. Time seemed to slow.

Then the feeling was gone. Emma looked down at her hands. The Heart's Blood was gone, too.

Everything sped up again. Her head spun, and an electric tingling filled her nose and mouth.

"I think I lost it," Emma said. She stared at her empty hands.

But the electric smell was growing stronger. No, it was a different smell. The dirty clothes she'd dumped in a laundry bag seemed to reek. Jack stank, too—of dirt and musk and . . . copper? Why did he smell like copper? She smelled the dishwashing liquid in the kitchen, the Chinese takeout in the trash, the mold on the ceiling . . .

"Well?" Jack asked. "Do you feel it? Do you have the Heart's Blood inside you?"

Emma realized she was on the floor. She felt dizzy, sick. Her heart was pounding. "I . . . I don't know. It's like smelling is more important than seeing. But I'm okay now. I think . . ."

There was a strange pulling sensation in her gut that made the room spin, and suddenly she smelled cats outside. There were so many of them the smell nearly choked her. Then came a deafening smash. The trailer shook violently back and forth. Papers and schoolbooks slid across her desk and crashed to the floor. Something shattered in the kitchen.

Emma felt more than heard the growl outside the trailer, felt it deep in her chest and the pit of her stomach.

"Jack! Who did you give the Heart's Blood to?" rumbled a voice. "What did you do with her? Come out here, murderer, or we'll rip this trailer open to find you!"

Emma grabbed hold of her bed and pulled herself up onto her feet, then leaned forward to peer out the window. Her heart nearly stopped when she set eyes on the mountain lion pacing outside the trailer, sleek and golden and full of murderous energy. Other huge cats came slinking out the forest and into her yard. Leopards, cheetahs, lynxes, jaguars, panthers, and, right at the back, a small tiger with an oversized head, sticking-out fur, and big, bright eyes. Only one of the cats was small like Jack, a round-bellied gray with long, tufted ears and a thick patch of fur on his chin like a beard. He sat gazing at her calmly, but she knew, somehow, that the weight of his magic was heavier than any of the others'. There were maybe sixteen cats in all. They sat, or paced, or lay down, but all of them, except the tiger, watched the trailer with a hungry intensity, their tails swishing gently over the grass.

"They can't hurt you if you're the Pride-Heart," Jack hissed. But even so, his back was arched, and his tail had puffed out to twice its normal size.

The mountain lion snarled, and Emma stumbled back from the window. Her knees felt weak and she grabbed at her dresser to keep herself upright. What had she gotten herself into? And here she'd been worrying about her mom killing her. She'd be lucky to live so long!

Then there came a horrible screeching noise. The lion was right outside the window. It held up a massive paw full of wickedly sharp claws and ran them down the side of the trailer. A strip of aluminum peeled away with another screech. The lion was literally going to tear the trailer open to get at them, and there was nothing Emma could do to stop it.

"I thought you said they needed a Pride-Heart to give them magic!" she shouted at Jack.

"If they have any magic, it's coming from you, from the Heart's Blood inside you. It's leaking out without you realizing it. Can you feel anything?" Emma nodded dumbly, remembering the pulling sensation in her gut before she smelled the cats. "That means it's working!" There was excitement in his voice, tinged with something else. Emma was too scared to wonder what it was. "Now get out there and do something. It's no good if the trailer crashes down on us before they even find out what you are!"

Emma swallowed hard, then stumbled out of her room. The movement and all the smells around her made her head swim. She was terrified, but for some reason she couldn't explain she didn't want to run away. Everything felt unreal. She felt light as air and strong as a rock. She wanted to laugh. She wanted to scream.

Instead, she raced through the kitchen, nearly tripping over Jack as he darted between her legs. Glass crunched under her shoes. Emma threw open the front door and jumped over the steps onto the concrete walkway. As she ran, she saw Mr. Simbi's tail disappear into his trailer, heard the door slam shut. She could hear birds high above, the soft swish of wind through the trees. She could smell the grass, the forest, the cats. Their scent seemed familiar to her, somehow comforting, like an old memory at the back of her mind, just out of reach.

But the way they looked at her wasn't comforting in the least. They seemed to be sizing her up, as if she were some kind of rodent, at best a brief, bloody amusement. She opened her mouth to speak just as the mountain lion pounced. For a moment she watched it in mid-leap. It looked majestic. Then it slammed into her, sending her flying face-first into the grass.

Emma rolled over and tried to force air back into her lungs, but two heavy paws planted themselves on her chest. The big cat's breath was hot on her face, and all Emma could look at were long, pointed teeth. Needle-sharp. Sharper than teeth had any right to be.

*I'm going to die*, was all she could think, surprised and certain at the same time.

"Where is it? Where's the Heart's Blood? Why do we have magic if there's no Pride-Heart?" the mountain lion growled.

"There has to be a Pride-Heart somewhere," the strange-eared gray cat said from somewhere nearby. "Since we suddenly have magic again after weeks without it."

"But it's not very strong," a leopard said. "I can't even hold my shape!"

"You could never hold a shape for very long anyway," the gray cat said, dismissively.

Then Emma heard Jack's voice from the metal stairs. "You have your Pride-Heart under your feet, Cricket. You might want to let her up before you accidentally become a Heart-Killer like me and lose all your magic forever."

The mountain lion yowled, then in one swift motion pounced on Jack. But something was happening. The lion seemed to ripple, like a reflection in a pool of water, and then shrink. The other cats were shrinking, too, changing from the large, wild cats to the small variety. In the half second it took the lion to reach Jack, it had turned into a wiry ginger female, with only the slightest tinge of lion yellow left in her fur.

There was a horrible screeching as the two cats fought and scratched and bit.

"Stop it!" Emma shouted, pushing herself up off the grass.

To her surprise, the lion called Cricket did stop, her gaze whipping around to stare at Emma. Jack took the opportunity to bite the ginger cat's ear, nearly tearing it off. Cricket spat and leaped away, then turned to stare at Emma again. "What is this?" she hissed.

The other cats all stared, too, still and silent except for the small tabby that had been a tiger. He was looking around, confused.

"Leave Jack alone," Emma said. She spoke slowly, hoping her voice wasn't shaking too much. "I . . . I'm your new Pride-Heart, and that means . . . Jack said you have to listen to me."

"See? What did I tell you?" Jack laughed. "She was right under your nose the whole time. I gave her the Heart's Blood so she could find her sister. Aren't you glad I saved you from being a Heart-Killer like me, Cricket?"

"The Heart's Blood was supposed to be mine," Cricket spat angrily. "And a human can't be a Pride-Heart. Give it back."

"I don't know if she can," said the gray cat. Emma glanced at him nervously. He walked over to her and sniffed. "Interesting. Very interesting."

"She's a human, Fat Leon. She can't be a Pride-Heart," Cricket insisted. "We can kill her and the Heart-Killer Jack, and put an end to all of this."

None of the cats moved.

"Oh, it's not so bad being a Heart-Killer," Jack said. There was a bloody gash on his side. He licked it slowly. "You all depend too much on your precious magic anyway. You've forgotten what you can do with just your teeth and claws."

"A cat's not a true cat without magic," Cricket spat. "Creatures like you don't deserve to live." She looked back at Emma. "I don't know what game you think you're playing at, human, but you will never be our Pride-Heart. The Heart's Blood is mine. It's not even working properly. Bits of magic here and there. Pathetic. The sooner your pet Heart-Killer murders you, the better."

Then she turned and leaped over the fence, disappearing into the forest.

"This is . . . unexpected," the fat gray cat said to Emma, "but you're just a kitten, aren't you? You need to grow up a bit, learn how to use your magic. Maybe then we'll be back." He sniffed again, and his tail flicked from side to side once. Then he squeezed through the fence and walked away, casually, like there wasn't any hurry. Or like he was deep in thought. The other cats glanced at each other uncertainly, then followed him.

Only Jack remained, and the small tabby with the crazy fur and the large head. "I've never met a human Pride-Heart before," he said in a surprisingly loud voice, bouncing up to her, then away again nervously. "I don't mind. I bet you'll be more fun than the last Pride-Heart. She hardly gave me any magic at all!"

Jack hissed and swiped at the air, and the tabby bounded after the others into the forest.

Emma sat on the grass. She was shaking all over. For a few moments she didn't say anything. "Are you okay?" she asked after a while, looking over at Jack.

He stopped licking his wounds for a moment. "I'll be fine. I've had sparrows put up more of a fight. They tasted better, too."

"I thought you said they'd listen to me," Emma said.

"I said they *will* listen to you. And that's true, they will. You might have to tear them up a little first, that's all. Nothing to worry about."

"Right," Emma muttered. "Cats don't worry about anything. Well, it would be nice if you would worry a little more about telling me when I'm going to be attacked by giant cats. I'll need to clean up all that glass in the kitchen." She hesitated, looking at the shredded back of the trailer. "I suppose I'll have to tell my mom and dad, sooner or later. I can't keep it a secret if they're in danger."

But she had no idea how she was actually going to use cat magic and a pride to find Helena. She didn't know where to start.

Jack went back to licking his wounds. "Let me know when you're done cleaning," he said.

Emma pursed her lips. "Oh, yeah? What're you going to be doing?"

"Sleeping," Jack said. "And once I'm done sleeping, I'm going to teach you cat magic."

*"Crags are usually blamed for the appearance of magic forests, but even crags don't know why the forests suddenly spring up the way they do. Of course, some of them might know, and just aren't telling."*

CragWiki.org

# CHAPTER 5

"Why do you have to teach me in the forest?" Emma asked.

They stood in Emma's backyard. She craned her neck, trying to see past the trees. Even in the middle of the day the forest was dim, the trees and bushes pressed close together. She couldn't see more than a few feet ahead of her. Anything could be hiding out there. There didn't seem to be any paths, either, no way of knowing which way to go. It wasn't like the park her family visited when they went camping, which was tended by rangers and had signs everywhere to guide you. "Can't you just teach me here? Or inside the trailer?"

"I could. But I won't. It wouldn't be right." Jack paced impatiently. "The forest is a place of magic, which might make this easier. The trailer park has crags in it, but it was still made by humans. Anyway, you're a Pride-Heart, you shouldn't be afraid of anything. Do you want to learn cat magic or not?"

Somehow Emma didn't think that Jack would care that she'd promised her parents she wouldn't go into the forest. *I shouldn't care, either. I'm a Pride-Heart now. I bet Cricket wasn't ever afraid of going into the forest.* She took a deep breath and forced herself forward, following Jack. He crawled under the fence. She climbed over it and hesitated a moment in front of the first tree, reaching out and running her fingers over the bark. It felt like a normal tree, nothing magical about it. She pushed aside the branches and stepped past it.

"There, I'm in the forest," Emma said, glancing behind her to check she was still in sight of the trailer. "Nothing to it, just a bunch of trees. Now will you teach me?"

"Well, I suppose this is better than nothing," Jack said. He jumped onto a nearby tree and clawed his way up to the first branch, seven or eight feet off the ground. Then he sat and looked down at her. "Lesson one. Cat magic isn't a trick. It's not just making people think you look different or making them love you. That's faerie magic. Cats only care about real things, and we don't care who loves us."

"What's wrong with faerie magic?" Emma asked. "At least

no one ever calls them crags, even if they are. They're beautiful and rich and they live in fancy apartments in New Downtown. I mean, I've never seen one or anything, but illustrations of them are always all over the newspapers and Helena's magazines. If that's a trick, I wouldn't mind—"

"No." Jack sniffed disdainfully. "Faeries can make some people see what they want. Don't you ever wonder why there are no photos of them? They make themselves look beautiful, sound beautiful, smell beautiful. It's magic, that's why they can't be photographed. So of course humans fall in love with them. That's why they live in the city while all the other crags live here."

"Does faerie magic just work on humans?" Emma asked.

"Oh, it works on other creatures, too, but not in the same way. Dwarves see them as humans with gold or silver hair and skin that glitters like precious stones. A harpy would just see a human, but wouldn't think they were beautiful, because harpies don't think anything is beautiful. And trolls, well, it's hard to tell what they're ever thinking. Look at it this way. You could use faerie magic to make everyone think you were a panther, but you wouldn't really be a panther. You wouldn't feel like a panther. You'd feel like you do now, as if you just were wearing a costume. But with cat magic, you'd have real teeth and real claws and a hunter's instinct."

"So . . . what do I have to do?"

"You have to pay attention," Jack said. "Cat magic is not just wanting things to be different. That's not magic at all. That's just stupid. You have to know. So . . . you're going to swing your hand at this tree, and when you do you're going to extend your claws. They're going to come out, because they've always been there."

"That doesn't make any sense," Emma said, wiggling her fingers. "I haven't always had claws, and they've never come out because I don't have them."

"Well, that's why it's magic, isn't it? Trust me, I know what I'm doing."

"Okay, I'll try." She tensed and tried to think about the claws she was supposed to have. Then she lashed out at the tree.

Her nails raked over the bark. She yelled loudly and clutched at her hand. One of her nails was broken.

"This is crazy. When's the last time you even did any cat magic?"

"That's not important. You never forget," Jack said. "Never." For a long moment he was quiet, and Emma thought he might have gone to sleep. Then he seemed to stir himself. "And that attitude is just holding you back. Now try again."

"Maybe your bad teaching is holding me back," Emma said. But she tried again. The results were even more painful than the last time, though she hadn't swung nearly as hard. She'd managed to jar her hand badly, too, because now her palm was hurting.

"If you keep thinking you're going to hurt yourself, you

will," Jack said. "You have to have complete confidence."

"What if it doesn't work for humans?"

"Well, it probably won't work for lazy humans," Jack said. "Think for a moment. You saw how your pride reacted when they heard your voice. They all stopped and listened to you. And I can see you sniffing at everything."

"I am not!" Emma covered her nose with her hands. Had she been sniffing the air a moment ago? Now that she was thinking about it, she didn't know. But here in the forest there was a faint scent of the heavy, dark wildness that she had tasted when she took the Heart's Blood.

"Your nose is already better than most humans'," Jack went on. "What did the pride smell like?"

Emma hesitated. "I don't know. It's hard to describe."

"But it was familiar, wasn't it?" Emma nodded, and Jack purred. "The Heart's Blood knows your pride, even if you don't yet. Stop stalling. Claws. Tree. Go!"

He was right. She had to believe in herself: She *was* the Pride-Heart, and she was going to learn cat magic, and she was going to find her sister. With a growl she swung hard at the tree with her right hand, then her left, right, left, again and again. The growl turned into a snarl, then a roar . . .

She stopped, out of breath. Her nails were a bloody mess, her fingers and palms scraped raw by the bark. Sharp pain throbbed in her right palm, at the base of each finger, like splinters she couldn't see.

Emma sat down on the ground, holding her hands against her stomach and trying not to cry.

"You can't be done already. It's only a little blood," Jack said. "We haven't even gotten to lesson two yet."

Emma glared at him. "And what's that?"

"All normal cats can change themselves. But only the Pride-Heart can change others. She can even do it against their will. Except for faeries, of course. But you'll never manage anything like that if you give up as soon as things get just a little rough."

Emma sighed. "I'm tired, okay? I was attacked by giant cats two hours ago, and then I had to clean up the trailer, and now my hand hurts and all I want to do is go to sleep." She yawned. She hadn't quite realized how tired she was until she said it. She could barely keep her eyes open.

"Tired is good. Tired means your body is trying to use the Heart's Blood, even if the magic's not working properly yet. You can drain yourself dry if you're not careful and you have to watch how much you let the pride take from you. The Pride-Heart is like a fountain of cat magic. Giving them magic will come naturally to you." Emma thought again about that tugging sensation she'd felt as the cats drew on her magic, turning themselves into huge animals. "But you have to be careful. If they take too much, you'll be too tired to move, and then they'll be useless."

"How do I know when they're using too much?"

"I'm sure it will become obvious," Jack said. "Right now we're working on claws."

"I don't see how claws are going to help me find Helena. You said the pride would help me, but they're not even here."

"The pride will come back for magic once they feel the Heart's Blood's magic again, but you can't depend on them to do everything for you. You'll need to be able to fight, too." He cocked his head. "If you don't want claws, you could always try giving yourself some proper teeth. Claws are good, but it's your teeth that get you the kill."

"I never said I didn't want them." Emma had already decided that claws would be pretty useful to have. If she was a crag now, then she was going to take advantage of the good parts. She just wished her hand didn't hurt so much. It was making it hard to concentrate. "I'd better get some rest." She took a few shaky steps out of the forest and yawned again. "Just a little nap. Then we'll try again."

Jack sniffed, but followed her. "Well, that's more useful than cleaning, at least."

They walked back to the trailer together. Emma climbed over the fence, wincing as her hands scraped against the splintered wood.

Mr. Simbi was in his yard, lounging in his hot tub. "Already going into the forest, are we?" he called to her. "I figured it would take you at least a week. You humans just can't help yourselves when it comes to magic. That's probably why you're all so scared of it. Like moths to a flame!"

Emma ignored him. He'd probably tell her parents, but Jack had said her dad was in the forest already, so he couldn't say much. That would mean admitting to her mom that he'd left Emma home alone. And her mom wouldn't be back until late tonight, maybe even tomorrow if she was offered an extra shift. Hopefully it would be too dark for her to see what the cats had done to the trailer, too. That was the last thing her mom would want to deal with after a double shift.

"Tomorrow was supposed to be Helena's birthday, you know," she said to Jack. "I mean, I guess it still is . . . Dad always makes cassava cake for our birthday parties. It's really good. But . . ."

But maybe Helena was dead. Maybe instead of a birthday party it should be a death day party, a *giỗ*, like they had for her grandfather every year, with incense and sticky rice balls. She really had to stop thinking like that. She *would* find Helena; she was out there somewhere.

"Cats don't celebrate birthdays," Jack said.

"Well, they should," Emma said, trying to smile. "You get presents on your birthday. It's fun." They went into the trailer and Emma locked the door behind her. "We can celebrate yours if you want. I'll get you something extra tasty to eat."

Jack laughed in his strange cat way. "Since cats don't bother with calendars, either, why don't we just assume my birthday is tomorrow, too."

"Deal," Emma said, yawning again. She couldn't remember walking into her room, but her bed was right there. She curled up on it. Jack was saying something to her, but it was too hard to pay attention, too much effort to open her eyes. She slept.

"Emma, turn off that alarm and get out of bed!"

Emma rubbed her eyes and sat up, blinking. Where was she? What time was it?

Her mom loomed over her, hospital smells still clinging to her.

Emma blinked again. Her alarm was going off. She didn't remember setting it. "Sorry, Mom. I thought you were working all night."

"I did work all night, and, if you don't mind, I'd like to get some sleep," her mom said. "Which means I need to get you to school."

School? How could it be time for school? Emma reached out and banged on the alarm until it finally shut up, then peered at the time: 6:55 A.M. She'd been asleep for over twelve hours.

"Thank you," her mom said. Satisfied that Emma was finally awake, she walked out of the room.

Emma poked Jack, who was asleep under her blanket and out of sight. "Why'd you let me sleep so long?"

"I was sleeping, too, you know," Jack said, yawning widely and showing off his sharp teeth. "Your dad tried to wake you, but he gave up after you tried to scratch him. You're a cat now. You'll get used to it."

Emma pushed herself out of bed. At least she was already dressed. She ran a brush through her long black hair and smoothed down her bangs.

"I don't know why you're bothering," Jack said. "Pride-Hearts don't need to go to school."

"Try explaining that to my mom," Emma said.

CRAG FACT OF THE DAY:
*"All books of magic sold on eBay are fakes.*
*Even if the photos look real, it's still a scam."*
CragWiki.org

# CHAPTER 6

Emma could barely keep her eyes open during the drive to school, but eventually she noticed that her mom kept glancing over at her.

"Your dad's making cassava cake and phở, for tonight," her mom said, eventually. She paused. "Are you going to be okay today? I know it's tough having to go to school and act like everything's normal." She sighed. "It's hard for me, too, going to work and thinking that she's still out there somewhere."

"Yeah," Emma said. There didn't seem to be much more to

say to that. Or maybe there was too much more.

Her mom tried to smile. "Remember last year, when Helena kept pretending she was expecting a car for her birthday, just to see how worked up your dad would get? She even bought one of those little tree-shaped air fresheners."

Emma nodded. "And she acted all excited when he got out his car keys to take us to dinner as if she thought he was going to give them to her."

Their dad had grumbled about spoiled American teenagers and how their grandfather would have cried to see what this country had done to his grandchildren. Helena had burst out laughing and couldn't stop for nearly half an hour. In the end, their dad had laughed, too. This year he'd been planning to get her a toy car as a joke.

Emma's mom put a hand on her shoulder. "Maybe we should have let you stay home today. You know, if you need to talk to someone . . . maybe your school guidance counselor can help you. Would it help you to talk about things?"

"There's nothing to talk about," Emma said. "Once Helena's back, everything's going to be fine."

They pulled into the school lot behind the other cars dropping kids off. "Emma, I know your dad still thinks he can find her, but—"

"I have to go," Emma said quickly, opening the door. "I don't want to miss breakfast."

She hopped out of the car and walked quickly over to a set of double doors leading into the cafeteria. Other kids stood waiting to be let in, and Emma took her place at the end of the line. She was glad she wouldn't have to see Marie yet. She wasn't ready for it, especially not today. And why was she still so tired? She'd have thought the Heart's Blood would have made her instantly magical somehow, rather than just sleepy. And it was getting annoying smelling everything and everyone. Didn't anyone here shower?

"What are you doing? Don't you know this is a human school?" Matt said, sidling up beside her with two of his friends. "Crags aren't allowed."

"Maybe I thought this was a crag school," Emma said, surprising herself at her boldness. "I just saw all these rocks-for-brains trolls standing around in front of the doors and figured I had the right place." She could tell by the look on Matt's face that she'd just made things worse.

"Yeah, you have the right place, if you're looking for trouble." Matt shoved Emma out of line with one hand.

For an instant Emma felt the taste of the Heart's Blood on the tip of her tongue. She smelled the wild darkness and heard the roar of a great cat. She hissed. She didn't know why. Somehow it just seemed like the thing to do.

It actually startled Matt for a second, too, but then he just laughed. He had the world's stupidest laugh.

"She hissed at me! Did you hear that? I think I should tell Ms. Keyes that she's got some kind of ratter disease or something."

"You better not touch me again," Emma said. "I wasn't a crag before, but I'm a Pride-Heart now."

"A Pride-Heart?" Matt laughed. "What's that supposed to be? Some kind of dork club you joined?"

More laughs. Emma felt her face grow hot. Her hand was hurting again, and everything she said came out dumb. But she kept talking anyway. "It's like a queen of cats. It means they do whatever I tell them, and I can do all sorts of cat magic."

They all laughed harder. This wasn't going the way it was supposed to. They weren't afraid of her at all, and they *should* be. Deep down, for no reason at all, she was certain of it.

Just as Matt was about to say something else, the bell rang. "I'll see you inside, Your Majesty," he said, and he hissed and clawed the air in front of her face, while his friends laughed. Then he went to join the main line through the magic detectors.

"Sorry, kids, you know the rules: No breakfast after first bell," Mr. Shuttleworth called as he closed the doors to the cafeteria line.

Emma stared at the closed doors as the few remaining stragglers grumbled and moved to the main line of kids waiting to get inside. It was all right if they missed breakfast, but she was hungry. She wasn't supposed to be hungry. She was important.

They should be bringing her food and hoping she didn't feel like . . . like . . .

Emma shook her head. Why was she getting so annoyed all of a sudden? She didn't even like school breakfast, and she'd skipped it plenty of times. It was just Matt, and her stupid hand, and everything else going on. She felt like taking a nap, too, and that wasn't helping her feel any less irritable.

She'd forgotten to worry about the magic detectors until she stepped through them. A series of runes began to glow a bright blue on either side, and the detector beeped loudly.

"Please step over here," the elderly security guard said. He took a piece of paper out of his pocket, and read from it. "Do you have any grimoires, spell books, amulets, charms, dreamcatchers, dreammakers, luck stones, holed stones, animal remains, or other items exhibiting or intended to exhibit magical properties that you wish to turn in at this time?"

"Does a chicken sandwich count as animal remains?" Emma asked.

"I'm going to have to search your bag," the security guard said, holding out his hand.

"There's nothing in there but books," Emma said, but she handed her bag over. She could feel everyone's eyes on her.

The security guard carefully laid her things on a small table off to the side: books, papers, old gum wrappers, one squashed and melted candy bar, and her old house keys. "Please step through again."

Emma did as she was told.

The runes glowed again, even brighter this time, and the beeping was erratic. Thin curls of smoke rose from the detector.

The guard frowned. "Must just be acting up," he muttered. "All right, collect your things and go on to class."

Behind her, she could hear Matt's voice. "I told you she was a crag."

Emma went to homeroom hoping that was the end of it, but of course it wasn't. By the time the second bell sent them to their first class, people were meowing and hissing at her as she walked down the hall. In second period, a girl pulled a bunch of hair off her hairbrush and threw it on Emma's desk, then yelled, "Look, Emma coughed up a hair ball!" Everyone around them giggled.

By third period Emma was thoroughly miserable. She never should have opened her big mouth, especially today. Knowing it was Helena's birthday just made everything worse. The teacher took them to the library so they could look up stuff about faerie influence on art during the Renaissance, but Emma didn't feel like it. She went to CragWiki so it looked like she was doing work and searched for "Cat Pride-Heart."

The school's computers were old, and it took a minute for the page to load:

*The Pride-Heart is both the leader of a pride of cats, and the source of that pride's magic. They are exclusively female. Though a few males have attempted to gain this status, there is no evidence that any have succeeded. The Pride-Heart also dispenses justice and protects her pride in war.*

She scrolled down and stopped when she saw the heading "Humans as Pride-Hearts in Myth."

*Nowadays, Pride-Hearts are almost exclusively feline (though cross-species Pride-Hearts have been seen on rare occasions), but there are numerous myths and legends in which a human, or part human, takes on the role of the Pride-Heart. One of the most well known is UGLY EMMA VU SMELLS LIKE POO!!!*

Emma stared at the screen. Someone had edited the article. The pain in her hand grew worse. She clicked around, trying to ignore it, until she found the edit button. Then she selected the entire article and hit delete.

*Click.* The article was gone.

But it didn't make her feel any better. She just felt angry, and the more she thought about what they'd done, the angrier she got and the more her hand hurt. *It's probably Matt. It's just the kind of stupid joke he'd think was funny. And now he might have made me delete something that could help me find Helena.* She was furious with him.

When the bell rang, Emma made her way to the cafeteria with her head held high. She got her food and sat down at an empty table. She drank the milk first and immediately wished she could get another. The fruit she'd gotten tasted weird, and she didn't like her fries, but the chicken sandwich tasted amazing. She didn't even bother with the bread.

"If you're so good at cat magic," Matt said from behind her, "why don't you turn yourself into someone that isn't such a dork?"

"Does Her Majesty want some milk?" said one of Matt's friends.

Emma looked up right as they all emptied cartons of milk on her tray. She stared for a moment, watching her chicken sandwich turn into chicken soup. The milk sloshed onto the table. She stood, trying to keep from getting milk on her jeans, but Matt's friends had her boxed in.

She wanted to hit him, to wipe that smirk off his face, to make him pay for making her hate Marie, make him pay for turning everyone against her, for her having to move to the trailer park, for Helena's disappearance. He should be afraid of her. They all should.

Emma tried to curl her hand into a fist, but she couldn't: The pain in her palm grew worse and worse — and suddenly she knew why.

Because a sharp, curved claw protruded from the base of each finger.

The pain was gone. The fear was gone. Everything became simple, animal fury.

Matt leaned in close. "You shouldn't be eating human food anyway, cat-freak. We'll bring you some nice troll food tomorrow and make you eat that, okay?"

Without even thinking about it, she swiped at his face, a quick flick of her hand. And then she felt her claws dig into his cheek.

Matt pulled away in surprise. For a moment it almost looked like he was going to laugh at her. His friends giggled. Then he reached up to touch his face, and all at once the blood began to pour out between his fingers. He started to scream.

"Matt, are you okay? What happened?" One of his friends tried to pry his fingers away from his face, but couldn't get a good grip. Another friend shouted for a teacher.

"What did you do to him?" asked someone else.

*Nothing,* Emma meant to say. *I was just trying to punch him.* But then she looked down at her hand. It was covered in blood. The metallic smell of it overwhelmed her. Her stomach heaved and she had to take a deep breath to stop herself from throwing up.

People were pointing at her, shouting, but she couldn't hear. *I have to put them away,* she kept thinking. They had to retract somehow. She tried to flex her hand, but the claws just twitched dangerously.

Mr. Shuttleworth, the algebra teacher, shoved through the crowd and pushed Emma aside. "Back off," he yelled, and he knelt beside Matt. "Stop crying, I have to take a look." He swore under his breath and pulled out his cell phone. "Everyone quiet down. I need to call the nurse's office. He'll need a couple of stitches."

Stitches? She couldn't have hurt him that badly. It wasn't her fault. It was an accident.

Mr. Shuttleworth was off the phone now and talking to Matt's friends. They pointed at her and made clawing motions. Emma tried to cover her bloody hand with her shirt. The points of the claws were like needles against her skin.

Then she felt a hand on her shoulder and turned to see the principal, Ms. Keyes, looking down at her. Her voice seemed to come from very far away.

"Please come with me, Miss Vu," Ms. Keyes said, and pushed her steadily out of the cafeteria to the main office. A cop was waiting for them, holding a pair of heavy iron handcuffs inscribed with runes.

"You'll have to wear them as long as you're armed," Ms. Keyes said. "We've called your mother. She's on her way."

"I didn't mean to hurt him. I mean, I wanted to hit him, but not . . . I didn't mean to." Or had she? It had all happened too fast. Her hand had felt strange just before she hit him, but not in a bad way. It had felt right. Hitting him felt right. If he'd just backed down, if he'd been afraid of her, she wouldn't have had to do anything. He made her do it. He'd threatened her.

The cop and Ms. Keyes were both staring at her, disgust on their faces. To her horror Emma realized she was grinning. What was happening to her? Was she becoming like Jack, like every other cat, not caring about anyone?

"Do you think this is funny?" Ms. Keyes demanded. "Because let me assure you, this is deadly serious. You're in a lot of trouble."

"No, I don't," Emma said miserably. "I'm sorry. I really didn't mean it."

"I'm sorry, too," Ms. Keyes said. "Now if you don't mind, I have to go call Matt's mother to tell her what's happened." She went into her private office, leaving Emma alone with the cop.

The cuffs made Emma's hands and arms feel numb. She fidgeted in the hard plastic chair. The cop kept looking at her like she was some kind of rabid animal. *Maybe I am*, she thought.

Emma's mom came into the office. Her eyes were puffy and bloodshot. The cop pointed at the empty chair next to Emma. Her mom went to sit down, but stopped short.

"Are the handcuffs really necessary? She's only twelve."

"I'm sorry, ma'am, but we have to in situations like this," said the cop, but he didn't sound sorry at all.

Emma's mom sat beside her. Emma tried to hide her hand, but it was no use. Her mom's eyes went wide when she saw the claws. "Emma, what's happened to you? Why didn't you tell me?"

Emma didn't answer. She didn't know what to say. She looked at the floor.

"What if you go to jail? Did you think about that before playing around with magic? Did you have any clue at all what you were doing?"

"They don't send kids to jail," Emma said softly. She knew that much.

"They don't send *human* kids to jail," her mom whispered. Then she started to cry.

The cop sighed.

"I'm sorry. I didn't know about the claws." Emma didn't know what else to say. She wished they'd go away so she didn't have to look at them. So that her mom didn't have to look at them. So that the cop would stop scowling at her. She didn't want to hurt anyone, they had to believe that. Maybe she could get them taken out, or filed down. She forced herself to look at them. Why was it so hard to remember what her hand had felt like without claws? She tried harder, recalling what it was like to move her fingers, to curl her hand up and open it again.

Finally, the claws slid back into her palm, leaving ugly slits where they'd pierced her skin.

The door to the principal's office opened. "Mrs. Vu?" Ms. Keyes called. "Please come in."

Emma, her mom, and the cop all followed Ms. Keyes into her office and sat down in front of her desk.

"We've just heard from the nurse that Matthew's eye wasn't damaged in the attack. He may, unfortunately, have scars, though she doesn't know how bad they'll be. As I'm sure Emma has told you, Mrs. Vu, we have a strict zero-tolerance weapons policy. The consequences of that are expulsion and a mark on her permanent record."

Ms. Keyes held up a hand to stop Emma's mom's protests. "I may be able to convince the board to overlook the weapons charge, since the claws are clearly part of Emma's hand: She couldn't very well leave them at home. So I'll see what I can do to keep this incident off the record, *if* you agree to withdraw Emma from school. We pride ourselves on running a simple school, Mrs. Vu. We're not equipped to deal with a . . ." Ms. Keyes hesitated ". . . child like Emma. I have the paperwork all ready." She slid a stack of forms across the desk. Her voice softened. "I think this is best for Emma and the other students, don't you?"

"But where's she supposed to go?" Emma's mom asked, her voice fierce. "She still has to go to school. She still has the right to an education."

"Homeschooling is one option," Ms. Keyes said. "There are also alternative schools for children like Emma."

"Crag schools, you mean," Emma's mom said.

"I never used the word crag, Mrs. Vu. However, clearly an all-human environment such as this is not the best place for Emma. Think about it, please. It's a better alternative than expulsion."

"Mom, let's just go," Emma said before her mom could argue more. "Dad can homeschool me."

Emma's mom glared at Ms. Keyes, then looked down at Emma. Her mouth was tight with anger. "We'll talk about it when we get home," her mom said. She turned back to the principal. "Just tell me where I need to sign."

A few minutes later, the cop escorted Emma and her mom out of the building. Only after they were off school property did he remove the handcuffs. "Don't let me catch you near a school zone again. Understand?"

Emma nodded. Her hands tingled with pins and needles as she tried to move her fingers again.

She and her mom got into the car. They didn't look at each other.

"It was an accident," Emma said.

Her mom put the car into gear and started driving.

After several minutes of silence, Emma tried again. "Mom, I'm sorry I didn't tell you, okay? I really didn't know about the claws."

Her mom wiped at her eyes with the back of her hand. When she finally spoke, her voice was steady again. "That cat's not going to get away with this. I'm going to call the police, have him hunted down. You know better than to mess with magic. Do you have any idea what could have happened if—"

She broke off as they drove up to their trailer.

There were cats everywhere. All of them were small now, but still they were all different shapes and sizes. Emma saw gray fur, white fur, ginger, brown, and black. They sprawled across the lawn and driveway. They lounged on the steps. A few even stared down from the roof of the trailer. Green and yellow eyes watched Emma with a still, stalking intensity.

The Heart's Blood was working. Her pride was back.

CRAG FACT OF THE DAY:

*"It's not a good idea to wear clothes made out of satyr fur if there's a chance you might run into an actual living satyr. It tends to make them angry."*

CragWiki.org

# CHAPTER 7

"Emma, stay in the car," her mom said, then rolled down her window a few inches. "Mr. Simbi?" she called.

Mr. Simbi's head broke the surface of the water in his hot tub, tail flapping wildly. "You have to do something about these cats!" he yelled. "I already told them to go, but they just ignored me. That's the problem with cats, they're rude and lazy. They shed everywhere, too. Look, there's cat hair in my water. It's unsanitary!"

"Do you have a phone?" Emma's mom interrupted. "We need to call the police."

Mr. Simbi shook his head. "I don't need a phone. And neither do you, because the police won't come here. They never do. Well, not unless they're disturbing hardworking residents with questions about things we know nothing about. But the moment there's any real trouble, there's not an officer to be found."

"Mom, I don't think they're here to hurt us," Emma said. "I just need to talk to them."

"Have you forgotten where talking to cats has gotten you so far?" her mom said. "You are going to stay in this car, and you are not to move until—"

A gray cat climbed onto the hood of the car. Emma recognized him from the day before, the one called Fat Leon. "This is not human business," he said, staring at her mom through the windshield. "We're here to see our Pride-Heart."

Emma's mom pursed her lips and slammed the heel of her palm on the horn. "I don't care what you want!" she yelled, punctuating each word with another blast of the car horn. "Get! Off! My! Property! Get! Away! From! My! Child!"

Fat Leon's ears twitched with irritation, but he didn't bother to move.

"Mom, stop!" Emma yelled, her hands over her ears. "I have to talk to them. I'm their Pride-Heart now!"

"No, you're a twelve-year-old girl," her mom cried. "And whatever that Jack did to you doesn't change that."

Fat Leon's ears perked up. "Are you hunting him, too? Then we want the same thing. He's hiding out in your trailer right now, like a coward. He knows we don't have the magic to tear it open, or he'd already be dead."

"No!" Emma said. "You can't hurt him. I order you, as your Pride-Heart."

Fat Leon licked his paw. "I don't think that's a very good idea. He's a Heart-Killer. You're not safe with him."

"Emma, what's going on? What's a Heart-Killer? Never mind, it doesn't matter. Just stop talking to it. We're driving to the police station."

"Sorry, Mom," Emma said. She yanked open the passenger door and jumped out. Fat Leon hopped off the car.

Emma stood in the middle of her pride. A faint breeze blew, and she smelled them all. She felt calm.

"Emma, get away from them!" her mom yelled.

"It's fine, Mom." Emma said. "They're not going to hurt me, right?" She glanced around at the cats. "Right?"

"Not if you're really our Pride-Heart," a thin black cat said.

"That's the big question, isn't it?" Fat Leon said. "You have the Heart's Blood, and it's obviously beginning to work on you, otherwise we wouldn't have been drawn here." He looked at her keenly. "Something just happened, didn't it?" He went on without waiting for her answer. "But the question is: Can you give *us* magic? Cricket said you're just a human, that we'll never get true magic from you, and that killing you wouldn't make any of us a Heart-Killer. But she's not exactly volunteering for the job, so she must have her doubts."

That was more than Emma's mom could take. She got out of the car and waded through the cats, ignoring their hisses. Then she grabbed Emma's arm and started to pull her toward the trailer.

"Mom, stop! They can't do anything to me; they don't have any magic."

More cats hissed behind them on the steps. Emma realized there were enough of them to be dangerous even without magic.

"Is this old human absolutely necessary?" asked the black cat.

"She does seem pretty annoying," the gray cat agreed.

Emma's mom sputtered indignantly.

"Yes," Emma said quickly. "Everyone is necessary! Don't hurt anyone or do anything unless I say so, okay?" She turned to her mom. "They won't leave us alone unless I talk to them. Please, I just need five minutes. It's my fault they're here—it has to do with my claws. I'll explain later, I promise. You can leave the door open, just . . . let me try to fix this. Okay?"

Her mom looked at her for a long moment, then at the cats. She seemed to wilt, as though she didn't have any strength left for arguing. "I trust you," she said quietly. "You have two minutes."

She let her hand fall away from Emma's arm, and walked up the metal steps and into the trailer.

Emma faced the cats. "I'll figure out a way to give you magic."

The cats watched her, completely still.

"Try it now," Fat Leon purred.

Emma swallowed and nodded. She closed her eyes and tried to remember what it had felt like when she first took the Heart's Blood. Feeling light as air and strong as a rock. Wanting to laugh and scream at the same time. The tugging in her gut that meant the cats were drawing magic from her. She felt all of it, for just a moment—and then she remembered her claws, and the anger she'd felt before she clawed Matt's face. She'd wanted to hurt him. That's when the magic had worked. *But I don't want that!* she thought desperately.

And just like that, the feeling was gone.

For a moment when she opened her eyes Fat Leon looked as though he'd grown somewhat, then he was his small, round self again.

"Well," he purred, "maybe there's some hope after all. A little bit. We'll do as you say for now, human."

"Emma. My name is Emma."

"Fat Leon," he said. Then he began introducing every cat in the pride. Emma tried to keep up, but it was just a sea of fur and ears and glaring eyes.

"What about that one?" Emma asked, pointing to the small tabby, who was sitting a few yards away, chewing on his feet. The only cat not paying any attention to her or anything else.

"Oh, him," Fat Leon said. "He doesn't have a name. We call him the Toe-Chewer. But what do you want us to do about Jack? We need to deal with him."

"You can't hurt him," Emma said. "He's my friend!"

The Toe-Chewer looked up. "But I thought he was a Heart-Killer? They don't have any friends."

"I have to go inside for now," Emma said. "But I'll be back, and I can try again." Though the thought of trying to get that feeling back made her feel sick. She needed to talk to Jack. Maybe he'd know what to do.

Emma's parents were in the kitchen when she went inside. Their voices were drowned out by the old Vietnamese pop music blaring from a tape deck on the table. The trailer smelled like cassava cake. With Helena missing, it was hard to imagine it being a happy birthday, but Emma realized she had somehow managed to make things even worse.

Her dad shut the music off and pulled her into a hug.

"I didn't mean for it to happen," Emma said into his shoulder, her eyes welling up with tears.

"We'll get this taken care of somehow," her mom was saying. "They can't just not let her go to school. We'll figure something out."

"What did you do?" her dad whispered. "What were you thinking?"

Emma didn't know what to say. She couldn't tell them she got cat magic so that she could try to find Helena. It seemed so stupid now after everything that had happened. But she still had to try, and she wasn't going to let anything stop her.

"I'm sorry," she said.

"I know," her dad said. "I know. It's just some cats, right? We can deal with a few cats. Like your mom said, we'll figure this out."

"Emma, maybe you should go lie down," her mom said. "Your father and I have a lot to talk about."

Emma nodded, not trusting herself to speak. She pulled away from her dad and went to her room, closing the door behind her.

Jack looked up from his spot on the bed. "I smell blood." He raked his claws across her sheets in annoyance. "I wanted to be there for your first kill, you know."

"I didn't kill anyone," she said, sitting down beside him. She told him what happened. "They kicked me out of school."

"Let me see those claws," Jack said, as though he hadn't heard.

Emma hesitated. "I don't know how."

"Oh, it's easy. You just sort of . . ." He flexed his paw and extended his claws, waving them in front of her face.

Emma flexed her hand dubiously. Nothing happened. "I got

angry, and then there they were. I don't know if I want them back."

"Why not? That kid won't mess with you again. Neither will anyone else, now that they know to be afraid of you." Emma couldn't help remembering that this was exactly what she'd thought, too, but that just made her feel worse. She really was turning into a cat.

"What if he'd lost an eye or something?"

"He has two," said Jack, staring at her with his single eye. "Anyway, he deserved it, didn't he?"

"I guess," Emma said. This wasn't the same as getting into a fistfight, though, or name-calling. You didn't get expelled for that.

"You don't really feel bad for him. Cats don't feel guilty. It's just shock because you didn't know about the claws. Don't worry, you'll get over it."

*Easy for you to say,* Emma thought. But something about the way he talked made it seem . . . not so bad after all. She'd proven her strength, even if it wasn't quite how she intended. She flexed her hand again, and the claws slid out with only a slight pain.

Jack peered at them critically. "Not too bad, I guess. They're a little crooked and you need to clean them."

"I'm sure yours are perfect," Emma said. Somehow, as soon as she was with Jack, things felt like they could get better. Easier. She flexed her hand again and the claws retracted. It really was pretty simple. "I tried to give the cats magic again, but it didn't work," she said. Then a thought occurred to her and she brightened. "If I can give them magic, does that mean I can give you back your magic, too? Now that you have a pride?"

"Once you kill a Pride-Heart, you can't use cat magic anymore. Ever." His tail flicked back and forth, and his eye narrowed to a thin slit. "But that's all right. It won't stop me. Not with your help."

"I'm going to tell them to go look for Helena," Emma said. "I don't know if they'll listen, but I don't want to wait until I can give them magic."

"You won't have to," Jack said. "I know just where you need to go next. The tunnels under the forest where the ratters live. If anyone knows anything, it'll be them. They have a way with information—how to get it and how to use it." He paused. "They might even be able to help you use your magic."

"Ratters? Are you sure?"

"Trust me," Jack purred.


There was a knock at the door. "Emma?" her mom said. Her voice was soft. "We're going to have Helena's cake now."

"I'll be out in a minute." Emma glanced at Jack.

"Go," he said, yawning. "We'll leave when it gets dark. Better to hunt at night."

"You should probably hide," Emma said. "My mom already wants you gone, and if she sees you here now . . . I don't think she'll be very happy."

"I don't see what your mom's happiness has to do with anything," Jack said, scratching at the comforter on her bed. "You have claws and magic. They don't. If you really want me to stay, there's nothing they can do about it."

"You just don't understand families," Emma said.

"It can't be that complicated. A family's like a pride, only you don't get anything useful out of it."

Emma just shook her head. She wondered if it was even possible to explain human things to cats. "Just don't let her see you, okay?" she said.

The look of boredom Jack gave her was the only answer she got.

Emma went out to the kitchen. On the small table was the cake, already cut into squares. It was a light, golden yellow and sprinkled with cinnamon. Her dad had made some spaghetti, too, but they ate the cassava cake first. Helena had always insisted that the birthday cake should be eaten first.

"Today is supposed to be about Helena, Emma," her mom said.

"But that doesn't mean we aren't going to talk about everything that happened at school. About what's going on with you. After I get home from work tomorrow, we're all going to sit down and deal with this as a family."

*Everything that's going on with me is already about Helena,* Emma thought. Living here, her school, Jack and the pride. But she didn't say that. Her parents wouldn't understand, not until she found Helena and brought her back. After that everything could go back to normal. They'd move somewhere nice. She'd go to a new school.

They ate their cake in silence. It was sticky and sweet and tasted of coconut.

"We'll have another birthday for her when she comes back," her dad said. "To make up for her missing this one. You'll see."

When they were done, Emma said she was tired and wanted to lie down in her room. Her parents didn't argue with her. "Talking things over as a family" meant her parents were going to decide everything first and then tell her about it tomorrow.

"Oh, and Emma," her mom called behind her, "you need to say good-bye to the cat. I don't want to see you talking to him again. Understand?"

"All right," Emma said, not wanting to start an argument. But inside, a part of her was thinking: *What* can *they do if I say no?*

She didn't want Jack gone, and not just because he was helping her find Helena. With everything that had happened at school, he was the only friend she had.

Jack looked up from his spot on her bed when she walked in. "Well? Are you done wasting time so we can go find your sister?"

Emma shushed him and quickly closed the door. "We have to wait for my parents to go to bed." They couldn't know what she was planning.

"Nonsense," Jack said, jumping down from the bed and standing next to the vent. "You've managed to give yourself claws, so now it's on to the next step of your training. All you have to do is turn yourself into a cat and we'll be on our way."

"I thought lesson two was turning others into something else?" Emma said, remembering what he'd said to her in the forest.

"You're not quite ready for that yet. Anyway, this isn't any harder than giving yourself claws," Jack said. "Might even be easier, now that I think about it, since humans don't have claws in the first place."

"I don't think I can," Emma said, shaking her head.

"Try," Jack said.

So Emma tried. She shut her eyes and tried to imagine herself as a cat, but nothing happened.

"Well, maybe the ratters will be able to help with that, too," Jack said.

"I need a nap first anyway," Emma said, realizing she could hardly keep her eyes open. "I've been at school all day while you've been sleeping. I'm kind of like a cat now, right?"

"Kind of," Jack agreed. "But you've got a ways to go. Did you tell those fools outside not to kill me?"

Emma nodded.

"Then I'm going to enjoy a little freedom. But don't nap too long. The longer we wait . . ."

"What do you mean?" Emma said.

But Jack was already squeezing himself into the vent, and a moment later he was gone.

*"Harpies have better distance sight than eagles,*
*but find nearby objects very blurry and hard to see.*
*This can make learning to read difficult."*

CragWiki.org

# CHAPTER 8

It was dark by the time Emma woke. She tiptoed down the hallway, through the kitchen and living room, and quietly unlocked the front door. Her pride still surrounded the trailer. Jack was sitting by himself by the fence, but none of the other cats had moved to hurt him. They'd listened to her. That was a start.

Fat Leon's tufted ears perked up when he saw her. "Are you ready to try giving us some magic again?"

Emma shook her head. "Not yet. Jack's taking me to see the ratters to see if they know anything about my sister."

"I wouldn't mind a good ratter hunt," said Fat Leon. "But you need magic for that."

"We're not hunting them, we're talking to them," Emma said.

"Pity. I suppose I'll still come along." Fat Leon stretched and kneaded the ground with his paws. His claws glinted in the moonlight, which seemed much brighter here in the trailer park than it ever had in Emma's old neighborhood. Or was it her eyes? Come to think of it, she *could* see more clearly tonight. Was she getting night vision, too? That would be so cool.

Jack sidled up to Emma and leaned against her calf. "We're wasting time," he said. "Take a few cats with you, if you want, but the rest will have to stay behind. The ratters won't like it if we show up with an army."

"Okay," Emma said. "Fat Leon, you can come."

He yawned. "Wouldn't want to miss out on any excitement after all."

"There won't be any excitement," Emma said, firmly. "Not that kind anyway."

"You never know with ratters," said Fat Leon.

The other cats hissed their agreement, their eyes glowing hungrily in the darkness. The little tabby they called the Toe-Chewer bounded up to her and batted at her jeans with his paws. "What about me? Can I come? Please?"

"No," said Fat Leon.

"Sure," said Emma.

"Really?" The Toe-Chewer's whiskers quivered with excitement.

"Are you planning to use him as bait?" Fat Leon asked. "I'm not sure he's good for much else."

"No one in the pride is good for much else," Jack pointed out. "You're all so used to having magic that without it you're hardly a match for pigeons, much less ratters."

Fat Leon hissed at this, his tail puffing out behind him.

"So, how do we find the ratters?" Emma asked quickly, trying to prevent a fight.

"Easy," Jack said, turning his back on Fat Leon. "There's an entrance to one of their tunnels not too far from here, in the basement of the crag school."

"Isn't the crag school in the forest?" Emma tried not to sound anxious, but at night the trees looked even more ominous, like they were watching her, waiting for something. She might be getting night vision, but it was happening slowly. She wished she'd thought to bring a flashlight for comfort.

"Not exactly. But enough stalling." Jack took off along the road that wound through the trailer park, Fat Leon and the Toe-Chewer following. Emma jogged to keep up.

The trailer park was quiet and still. The only sounds were the rattle and hum of window air conditioners and the scraping of Emma's shoes on the concrete as she ran. Old streetlamps gave off yellow, uneven light, creating flickering shadows. The cats moved silently, like shadows themselves.

They left the trailer park and followed a well-worn path along the forest's edge. Emma concentrated on keeping up, on not tripping over rocks or her own feet. She lost track of how long they ran. Maybe half an hour, maybe more. She should be tired, she thought, but somehow she wasn't.

Jack slowed to a walk as a derelict brick building came into view. It was two stories tall, with regularly spaced windows that were occasionally missing glass. A large tree grew out of one wall.

At first Emma thought it must be abandoned, some old place that just happened to be a few yards too close to Old Downtown when the forest started to grow. But then she saw the dirt paths that had been made through the knee-high grass, and the weathered signboard reading WELCOME TO HOLLOW TREE ACADEMY! Then below, in smaller letters: SPRING SOCCER TRYOUTS START IN MAY.

"Wait a second," she said. "You said the entrance to the ratter tunnels is in the basement. Are we going to have to break into the school?"

"Unless you have a better idea," Jack said.

"If we could use our magic, we could turn into something really small to fit under the door," said the Toe-Chewer. "Like beetles! I always wanted to try turning into a beetle, but our last Pride-Heart never let me use enough magic. I think—"

"Quiet," Jack hissed. "There's someone here."

The Toe-Chewer shut up, then chewed on his foot in agitation.

Emma listened. She could just hear a faint hissing sound coming from somewhere nearby. And a voice, muttering softly, too low for Emma to make out any words.

Her cats crept forward, low to the ground. Emma waded through the grass after them, trying to move just as quietly. The sound was coming from the back of the building, past an old chain-link fence that surrounded a playground. Emma squeezed through a gap in the fence, then stopped.

Before her stood a huge bird with an olive-skinned human face and long black hair. A harpy. She was as tall as Emma, but her spread wings were twice that in length, and she was wearing a pair of bulky goggles. One clawed, three-toed foot dug into the ground while the other was held straight out in front, clutching a bottle of spray paint. It hissed, and a green curve appeared on the brick wall.

The harpy looked so ridiculous that Emma had to stifle a laugh, which just made her snort instead.

"*Argh!*" the harpy shrieked, leaping up into the air, wings beating frantically.

The sound was horrible. It seemed to cut right through Emma's ears and into her skull, where it echoed painfully even as she clutched her ears as hard as she could. Distantly, she could hear the cats yowling in pain.

When the agony finally subsided, Emma found she was kneeling, her head pressed into the grass.

"You shouldn't sneak up on a harpy, so it's your fault you got hurt," came a voice from above her.

Emma's skull ached with the echo of the screech, but the pain didn't return. She looked up to see the harpy perching atop the fence, her goggles on top of her head. Her eyes were strangely flat with pale yellow irises and large black pupils.

"What are you doing here anyway? Is Mrs. Douglas hiring cats to guard the school, or something? If you turn me in I'll follow you around singing, don't think I won't."

"What? No! We're, um . . ." Emma trailed off, not sure if she should admit what they were doing. Then again, she didn't want to upset the harpy and set her to screaming again. "We're trying to get into the ratter tunnel. Below the school."

The harpy considered this. "If there's a ratter tunnel under the school, then why don't all the ratter kids use it instead of walking in the street, huh?"

"Just stay out of our way, harpy," Jack spat.

The harpy stuck her tongue out. "So are you going to break in? If you're going to smash a window, you should try one of those." She waved a wing toward a row of windows. "The first one's Mrs. Douglas's office. But you can't tell anyone I was here because if you do I'll tell them you broke a window."

"You don't even know who I am," Emma said, standing up and brushing the grass from her legs and arms.

"I bet I do. You're that human girl that moved into the trailer park. It's all over the school. Except . . ." she hesitated and squinted at Emma ". . . you don't look exactly human. You're a little blurry, and if I squint, maybe you're a cat." She blinked and shook her head. "Weird."

"I'm a Pride-Heart," Emma said. "So I have cat magic, kind of."

The harpy laughed. "How do you 'kind of' have magic? Is that like 'kind of' being able to fly, until you hit the ground?"

"No, it means I'm not sure exactly how to use it yet."

"There's nothing to know," Fat Leon said from behind Emma. He sighed. "It should come naturally to a Pride-Heart. It's too bad. With magic I could leap up on that fence and teach that harpy some respect for cats."

"Oh, quit your yowling," the harpy said, rolling her eyes. "I'd just fly higher if you did. Everyone knows cats can't fly. Then I'd scream, and then *you'd* scream, and what would that get you? Another headache, that's what."

"Let me guess," Emma said. "Harpies don't like cats?"

"I heard that harpies don't like anyone," the Toe-Chewer said. "Not even other harpies."

"Other harpies are boring," the harpy said. "They don't even watch TV or anything. They're all like, 'Chloe, why are you doing that?' and 'What's a gnomebot? What's a bot? I once saw a gnome and he didn't have metal arms.' Super. Annoying."

"Wait," Emma said. "You watch *Gnomebots*?"

"When I can." Chloe shrugged. "The reception on the cathedral roof's pretty good, but I have to watch it on this tiny portable TV. And I can't see well up close so I have to watch it with these stupid goggles on. It's easier to watch it from a distance through people's windows and listen with the portable, but sometimes they don't have it on or they close the blinds."

"I always watch it," Emma said. "I could keep the blinds up if you promise not to annoy my cats. Or my mom."

Chloe grinned, her face lighting up. "Deal! I don't turn you in; you keep the blinds open when you're watching *Gnomebots*."

Emma couldn't help smiling. "I thought the deal was that I didn't tell about what you wrote all over the wall?" She glanced back at it. The wall read Hclou tnec Tnols nave funq before cutting off mid-letter. "What's it supposed to say anyway?"

"What? What do you mean? I thought most humans could read." The harpy put her goggles back on and looked at the wall, too. She swore loudly. Emma flinched and covered her ears. Her cats yowled again.

Chloe hopped along the fence, beating her wings, her talons slicing through some of the links. "All that for nothing! You know how hard it was to get this worthless spray paint?" She stopped and glared at the wall over her shoulder, her head turning almost completely around, like an owl's. "It was supposed to say 'Hollow Tree trolls have fungus on their heads.'"

"Oh. Do trolls not like having fungus on their heads?" Emma asked. "I thought they always had things growing on them."

"Don't you know anything about trolls?" the harpy said.

"Only what I read on CragWiki," Emma said.

"Trust me, don't ever tell a regular troll he has fungus on him. Not unless you can fly away. And don't tell a wild troll anything, because they're not nearly as friendly and sane as regular trolls."

"Thanks," Emma said. "I'll remember that."

"Enough talking," Jack said. "We have ratters to find."

"We're going." Emma waved to the harpy. "Maybe I'll see you when *Gnomebots* is on?"

"Don't let the ratters gnaw you to death or anything, cat-girl." Chloe glanced at the wall again, then shrugged and raised her wings. She jumped off the fence, and her wings flapped until she rose into the air and flew off.

Emma looked over at her cats. "Ready?"

"You talk too much," Fat Leon said. "Let's go."

\* \* \*

Emma tried the nearest door, but it was locked. She looked back at the row of windows Chloe had pointed out. She'd just have to break one.

She pressed her face against the farthest window. It had been a classroom once. A cracked chalkboard covered one wall, and a few rusted chairs and desks were strewn around the room. Mold dotted the edges of the window frame.

"You're stalling again," Jack said behind her.

Before she could talk herself out of it, Emma picked up a large rock and hurled it through the window. The glass shattered with a crash, splinters tinkling as they fell to the floor inside. Emma brushed away the broken shards on the windowsill, then pulled herself up, reached through, and unlocked the window. She crawled into the classroom, then held the window open for her cats. They leaped in after her.

"We're in. This way," Jack said, leading them down the hall.

Emma glanced through other doors as they passed. Most of the classrooms weren't in nearly as bad a shape as the one they'd climbed in through, but only half of them seemed to get any regular use.

There were posters on the walls, but not like the ones at Emma's school. These posters were all about crags. One was a drawing of a troll—completely bare, all clay and stone and gemstones—wearing a fireman's helmet and carrying a child from a burning building. "We All Have A Place!" the caption declared. Emma couldn't remember ever hearing about trolls working as firemen. Another poster showed ratters proudly wearing business suits: "It's Great To Be Normal!" The artist had left out their massive teeth so they didn't look as scary as the pictures on CragWiki.

They came to a stairwell. Thick, gnarled trees had taken root in several places. Emma picked her way carefully down into the school's basement, and found herself in a large room piled high with old desks and chairs and rotting sports gear. Past the piles of junk were pipes and boilers and electrical boxes overflowing with worn-looking cables that had been patched several times over. Wires ran into the walls and along the ceiling.

"Here we are," Jack said. He padded over to the pile of sports junk. "Just on the other side here. You'll have to do a little digging."

Somehow, Emma had imagined that finding Helena would involve less digging through moldy basketballs and more magic. So far the only thing magic had gotten her was being kicked out of school. She flexed her hand again, extending and retracting her claws. It felt natural now. In fact, the thought of not having claws felt unreal. Like thinking about what it would be like to lose an arm.

She tossed aside bats and balls until she reached a large hole in the wall that led away into the darkness. Thick bundles of black power cables ran from the basement into the tunnel. The ratters must be stealing electricity from the school.

"I'd feel better about going in here if we could use our magic for real," Fat Leon said quietly.

"I'm sorry," said Emma. "I'm trying."

"You might succeed sooner than you think," Jack purred.

The tunnel was made of dirt, and was so cramped that Emma had to crawl as she followed Jack. It angled down slightly and turned often. Even with her beginners' night vision she felt nearly blind, but it was only that there was nothing to see except roots. They were everywhere around her, some growing into the tunnel itself. The air smelled like sewage, and Emma heard a trickle of water over stone, though the ground was mostly dry with just a few puddles of what looked like brackish rainwater.

The cramped tunnel opened up into a large sewer system. Emma stood and brushed off her jeans.

"Do the ratters live in the sewers?" she asked, trying to breathe through her sleeve. It didn't really help. "Doesn't the smell bother them?"

"The old sewers just happen to run underneath most of the forest," Jack said. "We're probably near Old Downtown."

But the smell of sewage and ratter was still overpowering. *Helena better appreciate this,* Emma thought.

"But see those cables?" Jack said. "That's how the ratters feed their machines to get their precious information. They hardly have any magic at all, so they try to make themselves feel better by mastering these little human toys."

Emma looked up. Metal hooks had been driven into the wall to hold the power cables up off the floor. There were many more cables than there had been at the entrance to the tunnel.

"I think this spot's good enough," Jack said, stopping suddenly. He glanced back at Emma, then leaped into the air, scrabbled up the wall, and slashed at the cables. They sagged down to the ground.

Emma gasped. "Jack, what are you doing?"

"That's going to make them very angry," Fat Leon said evenly. He gave Jack a sidelong look.

"That's the point." Jack sat down. He looked as if he were waiting. "They'll send at least ten ratters. They scout in groups, you know. But you'll have a better chance fighting them here than in their nest."

Emma felt her stomach drop. "Fight ten ratters? But I just wanted to talk to them."

"Then you'd better make sure to keep one of them alive to talk to," Jack said. "You'll *have* to use your magic now."

A horrible realization was creeping up on Emma. She could feel it even though she didn't want to. "You meant to do this the whole time. You lied to me."

"I didn't lie. I thought we were looking for your sister," the Toe-Chewer said miserably. He gnawed on his front paw. "And I'll try to help you fight the ratters! But I don't know if I'll be much good without magic."

"You wouldn't be much good *with* magic, either," Fat Leon said dismissively. "Although I hardly think we should be surprised that a Heart-Killer kept us all in the dark."

"Lying is something humans care about," Jack said to Emma. "But the ratters wouldn't have talked to you anyway. They don't like cats much. We're still going to find out about your sister, but we might just have to claw the information out of them. I'll be right here to help you." He crouched low to the ground, muscles tense. "I know you can do it. You just need the right motivation. A Pride-Heart isn't afraid of a measly pack of ratters."

Emma turned as a skittering sound echoed through the tunnels. Her heart began to beat faster. It was the sound of many clawed feet scraping over cement, and it was growing louder.

*"Ratters have been popular as spies for hundreds of years due to their excellent hearing and ability to tunnel. Even so, they find the term 'rat someone out' very offensive."*
CragWiki.org

# CHAPTER 9

How long did she have before they came at her? Her heart was really racing now, and her claws on both hands were extended, though she couldn't remember bringing them out. At least the Heart's Blood was still a part of her. At least she had her claws, even if she didn't know how to use cat magic.

"I'm not going to fight them," Emma said. "I don't want to hurt anyone. I just want to talk to them so I can find my sister." But that was a lie. Something inside her did want to fight, just as she'd wanted to hurt Matt, and that scared her almost as much as the ratters. She'd never felt like that before.

"What if you turned them into little mice?" the Toe-Chewer suggested. "That doesn't hurt. At least, I don't think it does. Then you wouldn't have to chase them if you didn't want to."

"Changing others against their will is hard," Fat Leon pointed out. "Much harder than changing yourself, or changing someone that wants to be changed."

"Then we could change instead!" The Toe-Chewer bounced excitedly. "We could be the mice, then they'd run right by us."

"She can't do it," Fat Leon spat. "It's no use thinking about getting magic from her. She's never going to be a real Pride-Heart. We need to get out of here right now."

"Too late," said Jack.

The ratters spewed out of a side tunnel a few yards ahead. They ran on all fours, a mass of fur and teeth and small black eyes. It was impossible to tell how many there were.

Emma turned and ran. The Toe-Chewer and Fat Leon were right beside her.

Jack came after them. "Act like a Pride-Heart or die like a human!" he yelled, his voice echoing in the tunnel. "You can beat them."

The ratters were almost on top of her. Emma's foot landed in a puddle and slipped out from under her. She crashed to the floor.

The ratters at the front of the pack stopped right behind her, but the others kept running: up and over the backs of those that stopped, jumping over Emma and the cats, and cutting off their escape.

They were surrounded.

Everything was suddenly very still.

Now Emma could see there were at least twenty ratters, maybe more. A few stood on their hind legs, their long pink tails held up above their heads. Their noses twitched as they sniffed the air and stared at Emma. A bright blue LED blinked in the darkness: One of the ratters had a small wireless headset taped to his ear.

"It's sabotage," said the ratter with the headset. "Cats. One of them's changed itself into a human girl, but that's all. What should we do with them?" He spoke quickly, each word a mix of chirp and bark. It might have been kind of funny if she wasn't so scared.

"I'm not a cat," Emma said, trying to keep her voice steady. "Just because I'm a Pride-Heart doesn't mean I'm not still human." *I hope.*

The ratter with the headset narrowed his beady eyes at Emma, then at her cats. "If you're not a cat, you could still be a thief. And if you came here to steal secrets, you won't be leaving with any of them. Our secrets are our own and no one else's." His tail waved back and forth behind his back, like a snake ready to strike.

Emma could feel the tension in the cats. They were ready to jump at any moment, she knew. Fat Leon's tail was puffed out to twice its normal size and the Toe-Chewer hissed at the ratters, a small, pathetic sound. No one moved.

The ratters weren't sure what to make of her, Emma realized. Her claws were out, ready to strike. She could attack now, surprise them. No. She retracted her claws and held up her hands. "I just want to talk," she said, hoping she didn't sound as small and pathetic as the Toe-Chewer had. "I'm looking for someone, and I thought you could help me. I wasn't going to steal anything."

"Thieves always say such things when we find them creeping and slinking, and cats only open their mouths to bite and lie," said the ratter with the headset.

The cats were done talking.

Fat Leon sprang forward and clawed at the leader's face. Jack leaped at another ratter, hissing and yowling as he scratched and bit. And the Toe-Chewer darted back and forth, swiping at the ratters' feet.

But there were too many of them. Emma saw the ratters swarm over the cats, then one of them gripped her arms with its clawed fists, and she felt something hot wrap around her neck. A ratter tail. Her skin burned. Not just where the tail touched her, but all over. It was like being stung by a thousand wasps.

This was all wrong. Her cats should be hunting down the ratters, not being swatted away like flies. And how dare they attack a Pride-Heart? Emma felt her tears turn to anger, and a surge of something — perhaps confidence or power — flowing through her body. She felt the Heart's Blood inside her. *The magic is here,* it said. *Use it.*

She had to do something. But all she seemed able to do was scream.

She screamed as the ratters tugged on her arms.

She screamed as her cats tugged at the magic inside her.

She screamed as a ratter bit down on one of her legs . . .

And then her scream turned into a high-pitched squeaking that went on and on and on . . .

The tail around Emma's neck flicked away, releasing her. The rat-hands gripping her arms let her go. She fell to the floor of the tunnel where she curled into a ball. Shaking, she ran a hand over her mouth. It felt . . . fuzzy. She felt her arms, her face, her legs. Then she opened her eyes and looked at her hands.

She had clawed ratter hands covered with dark brown fur.

The ratters stared down at her.

The Toe-Chewer was still hissing as he hung from a ratter's claws by the scruff of his neck. Fat Leon and Jack had been backed into a corner.

"Turning yourself into a ratter wasn't quite what I had in mind," Jack said. He sounded amused. "But I was right. Look at the progress you've made."

"Clever cat trick," whispered the lead ratter. But he seemed uncertain.

"We've never seen a cat turn into one of us before," one of the other ratters said. "It even smells right. And look at its tail!"

Emma found herself turning until she faced completely backward and was peering down at her own furry butt. There was the tail, long and pink, stretched out behind her.

"Cat and human and now ratter. The ratterking will want her secrets," she heard a ratter say. "Let's take her to him." Clawed hands were grabbing her again, gripping her hands and feet and lifting her up above their heads to carry her. She tried to scratch them, but her arms and legs weren't the same length anymore, her claws not as sharp. She didn't know how to move in this body. *I should have bitten them,* she thought, feeling massive front teeth with the tip of her tongue.

"Why will the ratterking want me?" she tried to say. "What are you going to do with my cats?" But she didn't know how to talk with her new mouth, and the words came out mumbled and squeaky.

She didn't want to be a ratter. She didn't want to be in the sewers under the forest. What if she never got out of this place? What if she just disappeared like Helena?

The ratters moved quickly. Emma couldn't follow all of the twists and turns they made as they scampered through the sewer tunnels. *We must be right under Old Downtown now,* she thought as they passed through a disused underground parking lot. Eventually they came to a wide basement of gray stone. There, the cables from the tunnel running along the ceiling and snaking every which way over the floor, fed into what looked like a hundred computers. A mass of ratters crouched over the keyboards, their black eyes bright from the glow of flatscreen monitors and flashing LEDs. They glanced at her, pointing and whispering among themselves.

The ratter with the headset stepped forward. "Do all the members of the ratterking agree?"

"Of course. They want to find out what she knows. She is of interest," barked a new voice. "Be quick, before she gets her senses back!"

Emma turned to catch sight of this new ratter, but as she moved an odd smell caught her attention. It was more than the smell of ratter. It was a mysterious, secret kind of scent, and it was everywhere—on the computers, on the ratters, on the walls, in the cables.

"Hurry! She smells our secrets," came the second voice again, urgent and hungry. "Quickly, do it now!"

Emma felt ratter hands on her tail, rough and unpleasant, twisting it painfully. A shudder ran up her spine. She struggled, but she was held by a ratter on each side and she couldn't get free. It felt as if they were tying her tail in knots.

"What are you doing? Get off me!" she yelled. Her words were clearer now, though her voice still wasn't her own. "Where are my cats? I'll claw your faces off!"

They lowered her purposefully to the ground and backed off slowly, watching.

She sprang forward, ready to run as fast as she could, but her tail was caught fast. A sharp pain shot up her body and she landed flat on her face.

Emma stopped struggling and looked up. She was standing with a group of ratters in the center of a huge U-shaped table, the kind she'd seen in offices on TV. Like every table in the room, it was covered with a mass of computers, and at each keyboard was a ratter. But their tails tied and twisted until they were somehow fused together. It was impossible to tell where one ratter's tail ended and another began.

She'd read about this on CragWiki. It was a ratterking, a bunch of ratters tied together that acted as the king of a ratter nest. Hardly any humans had ever even seen one. At least, hardly any humans had seen one and told someone about it afterward.

All this Emma remembered in the moment before she looked down to see her own tail knotted together with the pink mass of tails. She was part of the ratterking.

*"Not much is known about cat magic, as curious researchers have an unfortunate habit of turning into mice."*
CragWiki.org

# CHAPTER 10

*It doesn't matter,* Emma thought, staring at the place where her tail vanished. *I'm not really a ratter. All I have to do is turn myself back into a human and then I can get out of here.*

But she didn't know how. Emma didn't even know what she'd done to turn herself into a ratter in the first place. She looked around. Most of the ratters that were part of the ratterking were ignoring her, tapping delicately at their keyboards with long pink claws. But the brown-and-white ratter closest to her was watching her, swiveling his head from side to side.

"Hello, Pride-Heart human-cat," he said, his voice echoing in her head in a hundred ratter voices. "Now ours, a ratter always. Be calm now, not too much fear. Safe, very safe among friends."

She could hear the noise of the ratterking now, chattering away just at the edge of her mind. There were so many voices. It was like a dream she couldn't quite remember. Or a nightmare, constantly filling her mind with quiet whispers.

"Gets better with time," the ratter said in a gentle voice. "Easier. Not so confused and loud."

"What do you want from me?" Emma managed to say.

"Same as you want from us. Secrets. Knowings. We have important work to do."

"What work? What use could my secrets be to you?"

The ratter made a high-pitched chirping noise that Emma knew was laughter. "That would be telling."

Emma looked away from him and down at her tail. She took a deep breath to steady herself, then grabbed it with both hands, wrapping her long ratter fingers around it.

She gripped tight and pulled.

The pain made her squeak, and her cry was mimicked by the rest of the ratterking. It felt like the skin of her tail had been superglued to the other. She couldn't pull it free without losing half her skin. Or half her tail. She couldn't do it; it hurt too much. She let her tail drop and sat back on her haunches.

"No, no, Pride-Heart human-cat. You have to stay and give up your knowings. Then you'll be one of us."

"I can't stay here," Emma said, sniffing. Her eyes burned, but no tears came. "I'm not a ratter, or a cat. I just want to find my sister."

"Ah, a sister. What sister is that? Cat or human?" asked another ratter.

She didn't want to let them into her head, but if she did maybe they'd help her and let her go . . .

"Help us search and smell," the ratter went on. "If she's hiding we can find her." He waved at the computers and the ratters working at them. "See? All human secrets belong to us now."

"And then you'll help me get her back?" Emma asked.

The ratter swiveled his head from side to side again. "Why do anything? The knowing is enough. The knowing is the sweetest part."

"No, no," another ratter insisted. "The sweetest part is when others know we know. Then we have power. All secrets belonging to the ratterking. All knowings. Human, crag, faerie."

She smelled something. A secret, sharp and bitter in her nose. *Not just a secret.* The ratterking knew something it didn't want to tell her. But she was part of the ratterking now. They couldn't keep it from her.

A man had come to the ratterking. He was blindfolded. She

couldn't see him clearly; the ratters' eyes weren't good. But they remembered his smell, and it was familiar to her. Her dad.

*"Please, I'm trying to find my daughter,"* he'd said.

And while he was talking, ratters had hacked into Helena's e-mail and her HangOut page, searching for useful secrets.

Helena had logged in twice the week after she disappeared, each time from a different library. After that, nothing. No online activity, no e-mail or HangOut, no sign of her at all. Then one quick blip on her HangOut account two months later, using a phone that belonged to some girl Emma didn't know.

The girl had posted some photos on her own HangOut page, but they weren't very interesting. They were shot in some kind of club or party. There were people dressed in fancy clothes, an empty stage, but the pictures were blurry and had been taken down from the HangOut page after just an hour. Emma wondered why. After Helena used the phone, the other girl hadn't used it again, nor had she used her HangOut account or her e-mail. It was like she'd disappeared, too. Who was she? Had anyone reported her missing?

And why had the ratters sent her dad away without telling him any of this? Worst of all, they'd kept looking, sniffing out secrets, and had tracked the phone to a building in the heart of New Downtown, a building full of secrets they wanted to uncover—and missing kids were only the smallest of them.

\* \* \*

"You already looked for Helena," Emma said. "You found where she'd used that phone. But why didn't you tell my dad?"

"He had no secrets we wanted," the brown-and-white ratter said. "But you do. You are useful, cat-girl. Help us find more knowings."

"I can't stay here." Emma felt suddenly desperate. "I'm not a ratter."

"But you're part of the ratterking now," said the ratter. "Why would you go?"

"Please," Emma said. "What if I accidentally turn you into mice?"

But the ratter just twitched his nose at her. "You can't even turn back into a girl. Stay. Safe with us."

Safe. Safe was everything Jack wasn't, everything the cats weren't. Her parents couldn't keep her safe, just like they couldn't keep Helena safe. *A cat afraid of her own claws* . . . No wonder Jack had dragged her here hoping to make her kill something.

She wasn't a killer. She wasn't the Pride-Heart the cats, and Jack, wanted her to be. She wasn't the old Emma anymore, either. But if she was going to be anything but one of the ratterking's tails, she needed to figure out what she was, quick.

"I don't want to be safe," Emma said slowly, as if speaking too fast might scare away the feeling growing in her chest. "Safe isn't going to bring Helena back. Safe is just hiding because I'm scared."

"Ah, Helena. Yes, she has interesting secrets . . ."

But Emma wasn't listening to the ratter anymore. She was listening to the Heart's Blood. She closed her eyes, and this time when she thought about turning back into a girl, she imagined herself with claws, with night vision, with a pride. A tough girl with cat magic running through her. A Pride-Heart.

She could do this.

This time the magic was there, waiting for her. And the change, when it came, felt like cool water running over her skin. She opened her eyes and looked down at her hands. They were her own human hands with her own beautiful cat's claws.

Emma felt herself grin as she looked into the brown-and-white ratter's shocked face. She took a step back, away from him, then stifled a cry.

The tail was still there.

She couldn't see it at all, couldn't even feel it with her hands. But somehow it was still there.

She didn't *want* to be here in the ratter tunnels under the forest. She was a Pride-Heart, not just one tail of a ratterking. She wanted to claw off the nose of the brown-and-white ratter. She looked down at the spot where her tail had been, where in her mind it still *felt* like it was.

Then she slashed at it with her claws.

There was a brief, bright flash of pain. It exploded in front of her eyes like a million white stars. But in another moment the pain was gone, and with it, the voices of the ratterking. Her mind was silent except for her own thoughts and a faint electrical crackle behind her eyes.

For an instant, she felt completely lost. Then she thought, *Helena's alive.* And the feeling of loneliness from the lack of ratters chattering away inside her head was swept aside.

Helena was alive! She was still in the city, in . . .

Where? The ratterking's memories were slipping away from her. It was like trying to remember a dream after waking up, but the harder she tried, the more it turned to nothingness.

"What's happening?" she demanded of the ratterking. "Why can't I remember anything? Why can't I remember why I know Helena's alive?"

"We warned you," the ratterking said. "Not so easy to steal our secrets and knowings."

A desperate fear clutched at Emma's heart. "No, please, you have to tell me. If you know where she is . . . if you know anything about her . . . I can't lose her again. Please!"

"Why should we tell you? What can you offer us now?" the ratterking asked.

"I don't . . . I . . ." This time the tears did come, but she wasn't paying any attention to them. The other ratters were gathering around her again. To kill her? To take her away? Maybe if she understood her magic better she could fight them, make the ratter-king tell her what it knew. But magic was what had gotten her turned into a ratter. She had to think. She thought of Fat Leon talking about hunting ratters.

"I can offer a truce!" Emma said. "No more ratter hunts. I will order my cats to stay away from you. Once I have magic and I get my sister back, maybe I can . . . I don't know. Promise you a favor."

"Interesting," the ratter with the headset whispered. Emma wasn't sure if he was talking to her or not. She felt a twinge where her tail had been, even though there was nothing there.

"Maybe, maybe," another ratter hissed.

"We don't need your truce," a gray ratter said.

"If you don't tell me where my sister is," Emma forced herself to say, "then when I learn my magic well enough, I'll have them do nothing *but* hunt you every chance they get."

The ratters surrounding Emma hissed and chattered at this, but the ratterking only tittered. "We'll take your truce," it said, "and we'll take your promise as well."

"What do you want?" Emma asked.

"We want to be there when you find your sister."

"I can't promise that. Anyway, I thought you didn't leave this place."

"You'll see when the time comes. You won't have a choice."

A shiver ran up Emma's spine, right from the point where her tail had been. But it was true there was no choice. They had information about Helena; she had to promise them something, even if she didn't know what it would be. She had to take the chance. She nodded. "Will you tell me where Helena used that phone?" She didn't let herself say *please* again.

The ratterking's many voices spoke as one. "500 Ocean Avenue. New Downtown."

"500 Ocean Avenue," Emma repeated to herself. *500 Ocean Avenue. I did it. I'm going to find Helena. 500 Ocean Avenue.* "Can I leave now?"

"Emma?" came Jack's voice from one of the tunnels nearby. "I'll scratch your ratter eyes out if she's dead! Human Pride-Hearts aren't easy to create and I've put a lot of effort into this one!"

"Yes, go," the ratterking said to Emma. "And take your cats with you. But remember: You are part of the ratterking always . . ."

Jack appeared suddenly. He darted past the ratters surrounding Emma, then stopped and stared at her, panting. "Good. You're not dead," he said. "That should make fighting our way out easier."

"We're not fighting our way out," Emma said. "They're letting us go."

Fat Leon and the Toe-Chewer came running in after Jack. Instead of fur, the Toe-Chewer looked like he was covered in dried mud, all cracked and broken.

"What happened?" Emma said.

He looked at her sheepishly. "When you turned yourself into a ratter, there was a little magic, just for a moment, and I got excited! I tried to turn myself into a troll so I could save you, only then the magic was gone, and . . . well, it didn't really work."

Emma giggled. "It's not permanent, is it?"

"He should be able to turn himself back once he has magic again," Fat Leon said. "Well, maybe he will. But never mind that. What matters is that *you* managed to turn yourself into a ratter, and that means you do have cat magic, even if you use it like a human." He sounded almost proud.

It was a long, silent walk back through the sewers. Emma felt tired. Not just sleepy, but drained and empty. When they climbed slowly back into the crag school, Emma was surprised to see that it was still the middle of the night. She felt like they'd spent days down in the sewers, but it must have only been a couple of hours. She could still get home before her parents realized she'd gone out.

"You had me worried when you turned into a ratter like that," Jack said. "I knew a little fighting would draw you out, get you to use your magic, but I thought maybe you'd become a lion, or give yourself some better teeth. A bit of extra magic to turn the Toe-Chewer and Fat Leon into something useful, maybe. But a ratter . . ."

Emma spluttered. "A little fighting? You think all those ratters were *a little fighting*?" She made herself take a deep breath. "If you ever do something like that again, I'll pull your whiskers out. One at a time. Then I'll grind down your claws. And leave you to the ratters."

Jack only purred at this. "That's more like it. Watching you get your precious Helena back is going to be fun, I think. Oh, yes."

"Did you find out anything about her?" the Toe-Chewer asked.

Emma nodded. "She used someone's phone and the ratters got an address. 500 Ocean Avenue. New Downtown." She frowned. "There was a photo of a party, a stage . . . No, it's gone again. Something about secrets." She shrugged. "I have the address, at least. We'll go tomorrow morning, as soon as I get some sleep."

"Yes, I suppose that's as good a time as ever," Jack said softly.

And for just a moment Emma could just make out the scent of secrets wafting off of him. But then she forgot that, too.

CRAG FACT OF THE DAY:

*"A harpy's scream has been known to cause nosebleeds, rupture eardrums, and shatter glass. It can even be heard more than a hundred feet underwater."*

CragWiki.org

# CHAPTER 11

Emma woke from a deep sleep to the buzzing of her alarm. The bright, golden morning light streaming through her window made her blink. It was time for school. But then she remembered she didn't have school anymore. She'd been kicked out. Everything that had happened yesterday came flooding back: Matt and the spilled milk, her claws, Helena's birthday, the cassava cake, the ratters and the ratterking. Jack.

He'd almost gotten her killed. Maybe he really was everything the others said he was. Maybe she was stupid to trust him. But hadn't he pushed her to use her magic? Didn't she finally know where Helena might be? That had to count for something.

She nudged him with her foot. "Are you awake?"

"No," Jack said, not bothering to open his eye.

"Well, wake up," she said.

Jack just yawned and adjusted his position, stretching himself out across her stomach. It was too warm to have a furry creature lying on her, but she didn't kick him off.

"So what would you have done if the ratters had killed me?" she asked.

"I'd be very sad," Jack said, although he didn't sound particularly sad. "And then I guess I'd have to go and find another human to rescue your sister. Do you think your mom wants to be a Pride-Heart?"

Emma snorted with laughter in spite of herself. "Do you have any brothers or sisters?" she asked.

"Of course," Jack murmured into his paws. "Three brothers, four sisters. It was a large litter. But cats don't pay much attention to that sort of thing."

"Do you ever miss them?"

"I told you, it's not the same with cats. All that mattered was that we were in the same pride."

"You didn't answer my question," Emma said. "Do you miss—" She stopped as a loud scraping sound came from the roof of the trailer. "What is that?"

Jack jumped down off the bed and paced in front of the door. "How am I supposed to know?"

"It's not another attempt to teach me magic, is it?" Emma asked, beginning to panic.

The roof creaked and the scraping sound came again, like something was walking up there.

Jack just stared at her, tail flicking back and forth with impatience.

She was scared. *Stop being a baby,* she told herself. *Whatever it is can't be worse than the ratters.* But thinking about what had happened yesterday only seemed to make it worse. There were scarier crags in the forest than ratters.

Taking a breath, Emma opened the door and walked out into the kitchen just in time to see her dad trip over Fat Leon as he rushed out the door. Fat Leon screeched and hissed, and her dad yelled, "Didn't Hanh tell you all to get lost this morning?"

The phone was ringing, but no one was paying attention to it. Emma wondered who would be calling them anyway, since it had only just gotten hooked up. Emma followed her dad outside, where he was squinting up at the roof, one hand raised to shield his eyes from the sun. He swore in Vietnamese, a word Helena had once translated for her. Emma's pride had abandoned their usual positions around the trailer and were milling around, looking up to the roof of the trailer with a kind of tense boredom, like they were ready either to kill or nap at any moment.

"Emma, get back inside!" her dad said as she stepped onto the metal steps.

Too late.

"There you are, cat-girl!" called a familiar voice above her head, though something about the sound made Emma wince. She peered up to find herself staring into an olive-skinned face with pale yellow eyes. Long black hair fell down to the door.

Emma took a step back, grasping the handrail to make sure she didn't fall. It was the harpy, the one she'd seen vandalizing the crag school last night.

"I remember you," she said. "Chloe, right? What are you doing on my roof?"

Chloe straightened up, flexed her talons on the corner of the roof. "It just seemed like the most convenient place to land. Anyway, you said I could come over and watch *Gnomebots* on your TV."

"I think it's a rerun," Emma said.

"So?" Chloe tilted her head to the side with a quick, birdlike movement. It was disconcerting.

"I guess I could try to move the TV so you can watch it." Of course, she hadn't planned to stay home today, not when she could be looking for Helena. But she wasn't about to say that in front of her dad.

Inside, the phone rang again.

"This is a friend of yours?" her dad asked.

"I guess so," Emma said. "I mean, yeah. She lives around here. Somewhere."

Her dad swallowed. "I think I liked it better when you had Marie over. Even if I had to cook vegan food for dinner all the time." He tried to smile up at the harpy. "It's nice to meet you, Chloe. Do you think maybe you can come down off our roof? I don't think it's really meant for landings."

Chloe blinked at Emma's dad. She took a few steps back, then peered at him again. "Is this your dad?" she asked.

"Yeah," Emma said. "Who else would it be?"

"Just like on TV," Chloe whispered. "That is *so* weird!"

"What's so weird about having a dad?" Emma asked.

"Harpies don't have dads," Chloe said. "It's just weird. You live with him and everything? Why don't they just kick you out? I mean, you can't fly, so I guess that's not a good test, but maybe once you're able to run around and stuff. Or drive. I know humans drive a lot."

"I bet I could turn into a harpy," the Toe-Chewer whispered, peering out from under the steps. "I could learn to fly and everything. Do you think she'd teach me how to fly?"

"You should start small," suggested Fat Leon, licking his paw and glaring at Emma's dad. "A regular bird. Something lighter. Something that can't talk, maybe."

"I could still be annoying even if I couldn't talk," the Toe-Chewer muttered, biting at his front paw. "I'd just chirp real loud from the air and you wouldn't be able to get me or anything."

The phone rang a third time. Emma's dad made an irritated noise in the back of his throat. "You're okay here? She's, uh, safe?"

Emma nodded. Safe enough. Probably.

"Too much noise!" the hag croaked from her window. "Cats is bad enough, now I has to listen to harpy squawks."

"Sorry, we'll try to keep it down." her dad called back. "I'll be right back, okay? Try to get her down off the roof." He went inside, and the ringing stopped. Emma could hear him talking, but he was facing away from the door and she couldn't quite make out the words.

"Is she talking about you?" Chloe lifted her head to peer into the neighboring trailer. "Why does she think you squawk? Humans mostly just sound like, *blaaaaah blaaah blah*, hardly any interesting sounds at all."

"I don't sound like that," Emma said. "And you really should get down off the roof. It's not like you'll be able to see the TV from up there anyway."

Chloe glanced over at the cats. "Your attack cats aren't going to try to eat me, are they?"

"Of course not!" Emma said. Then she added, "At least, not if I tell them not to."

"It's okay, I could probably take them anyway," Chloe said. Then she spread her massive wings and started flapping. The wind blew Emma's hair into her face, and she had to turn away as Chloe maneuvered down onto the grass.

The hag sniffed the air and squinted at Emma. "So we has harpy friend now? And I smells ratter magic on you. Too much magic too quickly. Lost in the forest, yes, lured in by something you want. Too bad it wasn't me."

"I'm not lost," Emma said. "I know what I'm doing."

The hag laughed quietly, and shut the window, melting into the darkness of her trailer.

"I didn't know hags talk so much," Chloe said. "Is she going to talk all the way through *Gnomebots*?"

Just then the front door swung open and banged against the railing. Emma's dad stood in the door frame, clutching their phone. "Emma." He sounded breathless. "I have to go back into the forest. I've got a lead on Helena. Someone who says they know where she is. I think it's the real deal this time. They know what she looks like and everything."

"Wait." Emma grabbed his sleeve. "You tell everyone what she looks like, remember? You made a hundred copies of that one photo." It wasn't like she didn't want this to be real, but there'd been leads before. Maybe she just didn't want to think she'd gotten herself turned into a crag for nothing. But the fact was she had an address and he didn't: 500 Ocean Avenue, and that was where she was going this morning. "Why didn't they just tell you where she is over the phone? Why do you have to meet them in the forest?"

"The person on the phone was probably a crag. A lot of them don't ever leave the forest, you know. Or maybe they have something they want me to see. Anyway, I just have a feeling about this one," her dad said earnestly. "This time it's going to be different. I'll be back soon. You can make yourself something to eat and hang out with your new friend. Just be careful, all right?" He seemed to realize he was still holding the phone, and he held it out to her. "You can call the police if anything happens. Make sure to tell them you're with the human family, or they might not come."

"Let me go with you," Emma said.

"No, Emma. It's too —"

"Don't say it's too dangerous! My cats can help. And I'm way better protected than you are." She extended her claws as proof.

"Sweet," Chloe whispered.

Her dad stared at the claws, and Emma realized he hadn't actually seen them before.

"You're definitely not coming with those things," he said. "They've already got you into more than enough trouble."

She retracted the claws and put her hands in her pockets,

suddenly self-conscious. "At least tell me where you're going in case Mom calls."

"It used to be a diner in Old Downtown, the Red Caboose. She said to meet her there."

"That was our territory until the trolls moved in," said one of the cats on the grass. "We'd hide out from the rain there sometimes."

"There were cushions on the seats," another purred softly. "I always liked the cushions."

"Trolls?" Emma said. "Dad . . ."

Her dad glanced at the forest as if he wanted to go immediately, but turned back and knelt in front of Emma. "Listen to me. I'll be fine. I have to do this. But I'm not going to put you in any more danger than I already have. You've been through enough, and I'm sorry about that. But this is what it was all for." He kissed Emma on the forehead. "Try not to worry, all right?"

Then he was off, jogging across the yard, climbing awkwardly over the fence and disappearing between the trees. Emma looked around at her pride. Their ears perked up as if they knew something was about to happen. Fat Leon stood and stretched.

Maybe there was a trace of ratter magic still in her. Maybe she was just more suspicious than she used to be. But something about this smelled wrong.

"We're going after him. The whole pride this time," Emma said.

The cats all stood and clawed at the ground. A few stalked back and forth in excitement. Jack strolled out of the trailer and down the metal steps to her side. She met his eye. He looked hungry. "Forest first, New Downtown later," she said to him, then glanced at Chloe. "Sorry we can't watch *Gnomebots* together today."

"*Gnomebots*?" Chloe said. "Who cares about *Gnomebots*? It's a rerun anyway, and I bet this is going to be way more fun to watch."

CRAG FACT OF THE DAY:
*"Newborn trolls are created from piles of rocks and dirt
collected by the parent. Some trolls only collect rocks they
think are particularly nice-looking, while others favor size."*
CragWiki.org

# CHAPTER 12

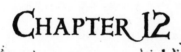

Emma paused at the tree where Jack had first tried to teach her to use her claws. "I've never been in the forest. I mean, for real."

"It's usually pretty boring," Chloe said, circling above her. "Just a bunch of trees. Sometimes you see a troll, but they're pretty boring, too. Even the wild ones. But at least you can fly wherever you want without a license. Well, I can."

"It's not boring to me," Emma whispered, taking her first steps past the tree. On either side of her the pride padded silently, Jack just a little in front, leading the way. She felt a strange pull inside her as she walked, and she wondered for a moment if the forest was somehow calling to her, if the Heart's Blood wanted her to go deeper, or if the cats were trying to draw magic from her. Probably it was just worry for her dad. She tried to ignore it. "How far away is this place anyway?"

"Not too far," Fat Leon said. "But we should be careful. Look out for wild trolls."

"Good thing you have me, then," Chloe said. "How do you even know where you're going? I bet you're lost right now, but that's okay, I know the way, too. I can scout ahead."

"Keep quiet," Fat Leon spat, but Chloe had already flown on.

They soon came to what had once been Old Downtown. Emma thought of the ratters tapping on their computers right underneath their feet. They walked past rows of townhouses, their roofs and walls broken by huge trees. A stream flowed out of one house's rotten front, cutting a path into the depths of the forest. Large chunks of broken asphalt and cement tripped Emma as she picked her way past the rusted skeletons of old cars. There had been a city here once. Streets, shops, people going about their lives. She wondered what it had been like for them when trees suddenly started growing up through their basements and floors.

"It's hard to believe this used to be a road," she said. "There's hardly anything left of it now. No wonder people are scared of the forest if it can do this to a whole neighborhood. What sort of magic made it grow so fast?"

"It's not just the forest," Jack said. "The trolls like the cement. They use it to make more trolls when they can't find enough stone. That's why there are so many of them now."

Emma looked back behind her and realized she couldn't remember all the twists and turns they'd taken. She was completely at the mercy of the cats to find her way back. Jack would stand by her, though. So would the Toe-Chewer, and maybe Fat Leon. The rest of them . . . she wasn't sure. She didn't really know anything about them. She couldn't even remember most of their names. Yet she felt comfortable with them around her: black, ginger, gray, tabby, cats of every color and size. And the smell of cats — her cats — was strong, overpowering the smell of the forest. A part of her knew she wouldn't have found it very pleasant a few days ago. But now it smelled like home. It smelled *right*.

Chloe appeared overhead again and landed on a high branch. "You're almost there!" she said excitedly, and she really did squawk a little. "And I think there's a troll there. You can see the grass all stomped down where it's been walking around. Do you think you're going to fight it? You should turn yourself into another troll and fight it. No, wait! Can you turn yourself into a gnomebot? What about one of their laser tanks? Can you do the laser and everything? This is going to be so cool!"

"Shut up," Jack hissed at the harpy. "That's the problem with you harpies. You never have to be stealthy. Just loud."

"I can be stealthy," Chloe said defensively. "I can be so quiet you wouldn't hear me until I was almost on top of you, and—"

"I can smell your dad," Jack interrupted, stopping. "He's close."

Emma breathed in. Yes, that familiar smell—of cooking and home. He was here.

"All right, so be stealthy now," she told Chloe. "Fly ahead and screech once if you see my dad at the diner and he's okay. Twice if there's anyone else there. Three times if my dad's in some kind of danger. But try to sound like a regular bird when you do it, okay? And don't let anyone see you."

"Got it, cat-girl," Chloe whispered loudly. She took off again.

"The rest of you, spread out a little," Emma whispered. She wasn't quite sure what that would do, but it's what people always did in movies. "Don't do anything until I say so, okay?"

The cats did exactly as she said. They were following their Pride-Heart. Emma felt their loyalty like a thread tying them all together.

Jack stayed next to her, his one eye flicking around. He looked tense. "I don't like it," he muttered. "There's something going on."

Emma heard Chloe screech once. She flinched. It didn't sound anything like a regular bird. "He must be at the diner now," she whispered, and gestured to her pride to creep closer, moving from one tree to another to stay out of sight.

Up ahead was a rusted-out gas station, and beside it a diner made to look like a train car. A massive oak had fallen on it and continued to grow at an angle, and a few of its branches hung down in front of the door. A peeling sign above it read THE RED CABOOSE.

Her dad was standing a few feet short of the door. "Hello?" he called out. "Is anyone here? I'm Chien Vu. I got a phone call that you had some information about my daughter."

"Don't come any closer, human," came a familiar voice from the doorway. Her dad jumped in surprise, and then Emma saw the small ginger cat in the doorway.

It was Cricket.

From somewhere above them Chloe let out two quick screams.

*What's that cat doing here?* Emma thought, just as the realization hit her. Her dad was walking into a trap.

She started to move, opening her mouth to shout a warning, but then a needle-sharp pain shot through her leg. She looked down to see Jack extracting his claws from her jeans, his eye narrowed. "Wait and see what her plan is before you attack. You don't want to run into any nasty surprises."

"If she hurts my dad—"

"She doesn't care about him. She cares about you. About the Heart's Blood." He looked thoughtful. "I didn't think she'd be so persistent."

Emma's dad approached Cricket. "Are you the one that called me?"

"I was," Cricket snapped. "But you didn't do what I told you. Where's the other one? Your daughter Emma? You were supposed to bring her, alone."

"I don't understand. What do you want with Emma? You said you had information about Helena."

Cricket turned her head back to the diner and called out, "Show him the girl."

A girl appeared in the diner window farthest from the door. Her black hair was streaked with white on one side, and she was wearing a trendy jacket even though it wasn't cold. She looked up and waved. She was smiling. Helena.

"Oh, thank God." Emma's dad waved frantically. "Helena! I'm here to take you home."

Emma stared. She couldn't believe it. Her dad had really done it. He'd found Helena, just as he'd promised. They were going to be a family again.

She realized she was holding her breath, as if breathing would somehow break the spell and ruin everything. But when she breathed out Helena was still there, waving at the window. The light on the window was dazzling, like sunlight on flowing water. Then, in the next moment Helena was gone, and the window was blank again.

Emma shook her head. No, she was here. Her sister was here. That was what mattered.

All that stood in the way of Emma getting her life back was Cricket.

She looked around, checking her pride was with her. They stood or crouched in the trees, waiting for the signal to pounce. She couldn't see Chloe anywhere.

Emma's dad ran toward the door of the diner, just as a large creature stepped out and pushed him back with one huge hand. It was a troll—a wild troll, too. Instead of clothes, it was covered in moss and grass that was actually growing out of its rocky skin, and a small sapling grew from its shoulders. It towered over Emma's dad.

"You'll have your Helena back soon," Cricket said. "But you have to bring the other girl. Alone, without the cats. They've confused her, convinced her to steal something that doesn't belong to her. The Heart's Blood. It's not meant for humans. It's killing the Emma you know, slowly turning her into a cat."

Her dad started to protest, but didn't seem to know what to say.

"I can help her. You'll have both your daughters back, completely human, and you'll never see another cat again."

"This Heart's Blood," Emma's dad said slowly. "Without it she'll be normal again? No claws?"

"Exactly," Cricket purred. "I'll even deal with the one-eyed cat. He's the worst of them all, you know."

"And removing it won't hurt her?"

"Of course not. Oh, a cat Pride-Heart wouldn't be able to give up the Heart's Blood so easily. But she's not really a cat, so it won't hurt her at all. If she knew that, she'd probably beg you to let her come here."

From her hiding place behind the pines, Emma asked, "She's lying, right?"

"Of course," Jack said.

"Probably," Fat Leon said.

Thinking about giving up the Heart's Blood made Emma feel strange. She couldn't imagine herself without claws now, without the smells, without the feeling of her pride. Would some of that stay? Would she just be the freak girl with claws that used to have magic? And anyway, did she want her life back, exactly as it was before? She felt confused.

"I just want what belongs to me," Cricket went on. "What does a human girl need cat magic for? Is this what you want for her, to live in that trailer park for the rest of her life, a place where you humans keep crags?"

*Just go, Dad,* Emma thought. *Go back to the trailer to find me, then I can take care of Cricket and the troll and get Helena back.*

"But you don't really care about Emma, do you?" Cricket asked. She sounded frustrated. "You let that Heart-Killer live with her. I can take her off your hands and give you back the one you want. One daughter for the other, an even trade."

Emma held her breath. It was a question she hardly dared to ask herself.

"You're wrong," Emma's dad said. "I love Emma. I love her just as much as Helena. If she was the one missing, I'd have done all of this for her, too." He glanced at the troll, then at the window. "And you're crazy if you think I'm going to bring Emma anywhere near you."

As Emma watched, a lump in her throat, he ran to the window and tried to push it open, but it wouldn't budge. The troll began to stomp toward him. Emma's dad banged on the glass. "Helena, can you get it open from that side?" he yelled.

But the window looked *wrong*. Emma frowned. The reflection of sunlight was back, but it was much too bright. Then Helena reappeared suddenly, too suddenly, and she was somehow rippling, like she was a reflection herself.

The troll was nearly at the window. Cricket leaped on her dad, clawing his arm. He threw the cat off, crying, "Helena, stand back!" then balled his hand into a fist, and punched through the window. Glass flew everywhere. He swore loudly and clutched his hand, then he stopped and stared.

Inside the diner, in the place where Helena should have been, was nothing but a bundle of twigs tied together with gold ribbon.

*"Most trolls actually stink far less than humans,*
*depending on what plants are growing on them.*
*Swamp-dwelling trolls are a smelly (!) exception."*
CragWiki.org

# CHAPTER 13

*No,* Emma thought. She stared at the bundle of twigs. *No. She was there. I saw her.* But she knew she'd only seen what she wanted to see. The image of Helena had looked wrong. She'd believed—wanted to believe—that it was her sister, but it had been a trick. She gritted her teeth. Crying wasn't going to help. It never helped.

Emma's dad blinked and rubbed his eyes. "Helena? Helena, where are you?"

Then the troll swung out its great arm, hitting him in the chest and sending him flying. Emma watched her dad land hard.

She found her claws were extended and she was running from the trees, followed by her snarling pride. She could hear Chloe screeching encouragement from somewhere nearby.

"Leave my dad alone!" she yelled, fury and grief and frustration welling up inside her.

"So he brought you after all," Cricket purred. "And you brought the rest of the pride, too. How nice. But they'll follow me as soon as I have the Heart's Blood—which you'll give to me, of course, to save your father. Or you can try to fight me. And then my troll will crush both your heads in and I'll have my pride anyway."

The troll took a step toward them.

"You've decided to become a Heart-Killer, have you?" said Jack. "I'm a little impressed. You were always so disgustingly loyal, I didn't think you had it in you."

This just made Cricket hiss and spit again. "Look who's talking. I'm not a Heart-Killer if I don't actually kill her!" She glanced around at the other cats. "She's not a real Pride-Heart. She's not even a cat. How can I be a Heart-Killer if I kill a human girl that harbors a murderer and is too stupid to stay out of cat business?"

But the pride was not swayed. They crept out from behind Emma and began to close in, tails bristling, green and yellow eyes locked on Cricket. As long as Emma had the Heart's Blood, they were loyal to her.

Emma looked over at her dad. He was trying to crawl toward the diner's front door, clutching at his side and sucking in air. She would make Cricket pay for that. She wasn't scared of her anymore, like she'd been just a couple of days ago when she'd pounced on her as a mountain lion. Jack, the Toe-Chewer, and Fat Leon were at her side, and she could see Chloe now, partly hidden at the top of a tree but ready for action.

Wild trolls were dangerous, though. She didn't want to put her pride or her new friend in peril if she didn't have to.

"I don't want to fight you," Emma said. "But I'm not giving up the Heart's Blood, either. Or my cats. Not when I'm so close to finding my sister." She hesitated, unsure if she was doing the right thing. "Why don't you join me instead? Become a part of my pride. Help me find Helena."

All of the cats stopped and stared at her.

"You'd never be able to trust her," Jack hissed. "Better to kill her and be done with it."

"Better to trust me instead of him," Cricket said. "Do you really think he gave you the Heart's Blood because he wants to help you? He's a true Heart-Killer. He only knows how to help himself! He's planning something, I just don't—"

Jack was done listening. He darted past Emma, running at Cricket.

"Jack!" Emma yelled, but it was too late. He pounced.

The troll moved like a landslide, faster than Emma would have believed possible. He grabbed Jack out of the air, then threw him almost casually against the wall of the diner. Jack hit it with a sickening thud, splintering the rotting wood, then crumpled to the ground, where he lay quite still.

Cricket jumped up on the troll's shoulders, and looked down at Emma. "You never should have listened to his lies," she purred, her tail flicking back and forth. "Kill her," she instructed the troll. "If she runs, kill the other human instead. The one-eyed cat can die, too, but try not to hurt the others. They're mine." Then she leaped onto the roof of the diner to watch.

The troll looked at Emma with small, ruby eyes. "I will plant your bones in my garden, little one," he said, his voice a slow, grinding bass that carried no emotion. "Do not be afraid." Then he thundered toward her, his footsteps cracking the cement underfoot.

Emma didn't—couldn't—move. She'd have as much luck trying to fight a mountain. Her cats leaped at the troll, climbing it and clawing it, sending bits of grass and dirt flying. But he just threw them off, and came steadily forward.

Emma extended her claws, trying to will herself to attack even though she knew it was useless.

"Claws alone won't stop them," Fat Leon said. He was still standing calmly next to her. "But magic will."

"I don't know how!" Emma said.

"The Heart's Blood knows," Fat Leon said. "And so do you."

A scream tore the air, a sound so horrible it seemed to cut through Emma's skull. She fell to her knees, covering her ears to block out the sound, but it didn't help. All around her, the cats howled in pain, scratching at their ears and rolling on the ground. Even the troll rumbled and shook his head. Cricket clung to the diner's roof, her eyes rolling up into her head, tail lashing out every which way.

Through eyes half closed with pain, Emma saw Chloe fall from the sky and grab Cricket in her talons. The ginger cat hissed and spat and twisted, scratching at Chloe's legs.

"Please. Help me," Emma whispered to the Heart's Blood. She shut her eyes. *Help Dad. Help Chloe. Help Jack. They're all part of my pride.*

Carefully, deliberately, she let her fear fall away and the magic take its place. She felt the tugging in her gut, and stopped fighting it. The magic flowed out of her like a great dam bursting, but she stood in its waters like a rock, still and strong and certain.

"Magic!" the Toe-Chewer cried out giddily, and other cats echoed him, purring, "Magic, magic . . ."

Emma opened her eyes just as Cricket fell from Chloe's claws, spinning in midair out of instinct, trying to land on her feet but crashing to the ground instead.

The whole clearing stopped—human, cat, harpy, troll. *Was she dead?*

Then Cricket began to move—and to grow. She was using Emma's magic, too, just like the rest of the pride. Emma didn't know how to stop her. The magic was for all the cats in her pride—and Cricket was still part of it.

The clearing was now filled with deafening roars as enormous lions and panthers and tigers replaced the small cats. Fat Leon looked like himself but ten times larger. The Toe-Chewer had turned himself into some kind of fox. In Cricket's place the mountain lion stood once more, her eyes on Jack, who still lay motionless.

"Help Jack," Emma cried to the other cats. "Don't let Cricket get away."

And before Emma could stop him, the Toe-Chewer bounded toward Cricket. He was going to get hurt—or worse. What could a fox do against a mountain lion?

*If I can give magic, I must be able to take it away,* Emma thought, desperately. She concentrated on the magic flowing out of her, the different threads connecting her to each of her cats, and with an instinct she hadn't realized she had she felt the thread going to Cricket. With a thought, she stopped it. Cricket yowled as her lion form wavered and shrank.

Emma turned as the troll bellowed behind her. Her pride had

pounced on it, digging their huge claws into whatever cracks they could find in its skin, trying to pry it apart. But they couldn't stop it. The troll grabbed one of the cats—a small lynx—with both hands and squeezed.

Emma felt a pang of pain and fear and anger wash over her, and then some part of her faded. Just like that, the cat was dead.

"It's not enough," she whispered. "Even with magic, it's not enough."

"You turned yourself into a ratter," said Fat Leon next to her. "You should be able to turn him into something, too."

"I can't!" Emma cried. Her cats were circling the troll now, but it was still coming toward her.

Fat Leon licked his lips as if he'd been anticipating this. "You won't have to do it alone. I can help. Focus on the troll. You're a Pride-Heart. Tell your eyes what to see, tell your nose what to smell. That's not a troll, just a stone. A big, broken stone."

Emma tried. She saw the world with the double vision of a human and a cat. She concentrated as hard as she could, in an effort to force out the magic inside her. Beside her she could feel the weight of Fat Leon's magic steadying her and guiding her, reaching out for the troll with her. The rumble of the troll's heartbeat began to slow.

*Nothing but stone.*

Slower . . .

She pushed the magic out at the troll, and the cats around her joined Fat Leon and did the same.

*Nothing but stone.*

Slower and slower . . .

This was the pride. All of them working together. This was what their power really meant.

The heartbeat stopped.

Emma fell to her knees. She felt suddenly numb. Beside her, Fat Leon was panting. "Well done," he said. "You'll feel better soon, don't worry."

"Is it . . . dead?" Emma asked.

"As dead as stone," Fat Leon said. "Unless you want to change it back."

"Hey, Pride-Heart, that was awesome!" the Toe-Chewer cried out.

Emma breathed a sigh of relief. He was okay. One of the other cats—a leopard—sat next to him, Cricket hanging from its jaws. Cricket had become a small ginger cat again. She was hissing and swiping at the leopard's throat. The leopard shook her until she stopped struggling.

The grin on the Toe-Chewer's fox face made him look slightly terrifying. "It's so much fun having magic!" he added. "Maybe I could turn into a harpy next, or even a dragon. A dragon would be *amazing*!"

"We'll see," Emma said. Then she remembered and spun around. "Where's Jack? Jack!"

"You worry too much," Jack said.

He was sitting near where he'd been thrown, calmly licking his paw. "You can handle this yourself," Jack purred, looking at Cricket. "Now that you're finally a true Pride-Heart."

Emma rubbed her face. She still felt numb from turning the troll into stone. Its head and arms had already broken off, the sapling lying on the ground. The cat that had died lay nearby, trampled and bloody, its empty eyes staring off into the forest. "Let me guess. You want me to kill her, right?"

"Unless you have a better idea for how to keep her from coming after you again, not to mention your dad," Jack said.

Emma's heart skipped a beat. "Dad!" She looked around desperately. How could she have forgotten about him? What if he was lying unconscious somewhere, or worse? Why hadn't she sent one of the cats to find him and make sure he didn't get trampled? "Dad, are you all right? Dad!"

Then she heard his voice. "Emma, I'm okay! I'm right here."

Emma's dad sat propped against the wall of the Red Caboose. She ran over and knelt beside him. His breath came in short, painful gasps.

"Dad, are you hurt?" Emma asked. His hand was still bleeding, and she could see bits of glass embedded in his skin.

"I'll be fine." He smiled crookedly and put his good hand on her arm. "I thought I told you to stay at home. But . . . I guess I'm glad you didn't. I saw what you did over there. You're not just my little Emma anymore, are you?" Then the smile fell from his face and he let Emma go. "Helena. Where's Helena?"

"Dad, she's not here. It was a trick."

But he wasn't listening. Clutching his hand to his chest, he dragged himself to his feet and took heavy, limping steps toward the Red Caboose. "Helena? Where are you?"

"You're bleeding," Emma said. "We have to get you home or to the hospital."

"She's here. She has to be here." Gritting his teeth against the pain, he walked into the diner. Emma followed him.

Inside, the Red Caboose had somehow avoided being impaled by trees, but the forest had managed to creep in all the same. Broken ketchup bottles sprouted strange, small flowers. Thin vines ran along the floor and up the cracked walls.

Her dad called Helena's name as he searched the booths, the burned-out kitchen, the ruined bathrooms. Then he returned to the table where the fake Helena had been sitting, where the bundle of twigs still sat on the booth's upholstery, the golden ribbon fluttering.

"Helena?" he whispered. Hesitantly, he picked up a shard of glass and held it up in front of his face. He started as if he could see her inside it, then brought the glass closer. He stared at the twigs.

"It was just some kind of trick," Emma said again. "Though how Cricket did it, I don't know. But I've found out something. An address where she used a phone: 500 Ocean Avenue in New Downtown."

Her dad shook his head. "No, she has to be here. I saw her. You have to look through the glass."

Emma snatched the bundle of twigs off the seat. He grabbed her with his injured hand without thinking, then cried out as she easily pulled free of his grasp.

"Emma! What are you doing?"

"I miss her, too, Dad. You're not the only one that lost her. Go home and let me keep looking for her, or this was all for nothing."

She extended her claws. Her dad's eyes grew wide, but before he could take another step Emma sliced through the golden ribbon. The twigs fell on the ground and she stomped on them.

*Crack!* They were all thin, dry, and brittle. *Crack! Crack!*

Soon the bundle was nothing but a small pile of crushed wood.

"I'm going to have one of my cats guide you home," Emma said softly. "Mom should be there soon. She can take you to the hospital. I'm going after Helena."

"Emma, you know I can't let you do that. It's dangerous. All this cat stuff has to stop. You saved my life, but you could've been killed yourself. I couldn't stand losing you, too."

"Dad, you can't stop me from going."

"You're just like your grandfather, you know," he said. "He gave up everything to get me and my mother out of Vietnam after the war. When Helena disappeared, I thought, how can I do any less? How can I risk less than he did for me?" He looked down at Emma and smiled sadly. "I'm sorry this happened to you. I would have done the same thing if you'd been the one to disappear like that. And . . . I'm proud of you."

"Thanks, Dad," Emma said, her voice only a little hoarse.

"If your mom asks, I yelled at you about going, all right?" he said. "I was very strict and authoritarian, but you just wouldn't listen."

Emma grinned, and blinked the tears out of her eyes. "Nope. I didn't listen at all."

*"It's estimated that only one in a thousand trees is awake enough to have a real dryad, or tree spirit. A law passed in 1976 requires anyone wishing to chop down a tree to knock three times before cutting, and ask it if it is awake."*

CragWiki.org

# CHAPTER 14

Once her dad had gone, his arm over the back of a tortoise-shell cat, Emma turned back to her pride. The cats were sprawled around the stone troll, licking their wounds. The Toe-Chewer stood to one side. He seemed not to know what to do with himself.

"So what are you going to do with the dead cat?" Chloe asked. "Do they eat it, or what?"

"No!" Emma said. "No one's going to eat it. We'll bury it. Him."

"What for?" Fat Leon asked. "He's dead. Might as well just leave him there."

"Because he was part of my pride," Emma said. *Because I felt him die for me.* She shivered as she remembered the part of her that had faded as the troll had squeezed the life out of the cat.

The leopard broke her thoughts. "I'm tired of holding her," she said, pinning Cricket under her huge paws. "It's no fun if you can't eat them once they stop squirming." The comment was delivered in the usual I-don't-really-care manner that all the cats except the Toe-Chewer seemed to have, but Emma realized they were waiting to see what she would do.

Cricket hissed weakly as Emma walked up to her. "You're a fool for trusting Jack. He probably knows where your sister is. He's probably known this whole time."

"Lies," Jack replied nonchalantly. "But even if I had known, you weren't ready to go after her, were you, Emma? Now that you have your magic, it's a different story."

"You think he's your friend," Cricket spat. "But cats don't have friends. They have a pride, or they have nothing."

"You know, I was a little disappointed your first kill wasn't one of the ratters. But I think killing Cricket is better," Jack purred. "More fitting."

"You forgot the troll," Emma murmured, extracting her claws and staring at them thoughtfully. She knew what the wild Pride-Heart wanted to do. But what did she want?

"It doesn't count if there wasn't any blood," Jack said.

"Hurry up. I'm sick of the sound of his voice," Cricket said. She sounded tired. Defeated. "They're waiting. Go ahead and show them you're a real cat now."

"But I'm not," Emma said. "Not exactly. I'm human, too."

She shut her eyes and felt the connection between herself and Cricket, that thread binding them together. Slowly, gently, she let the magic flow into the ginger cat again. Cricket looked up at her, puzzled. Then she turned into the mountain lion once more.

"Stop her!" Jack yelled. He sounded furious.

The others cats didn't move. They all watched Emma.

Cricket looked around as if she wanted to run, but she stayed where she was. "I won't be hunted just to amuse you," she growled.

"I don't want to hunt you," Emma said. "I want you by my side. You're no Heart-Killer. Not really. Like Jack said, you don't have it in you."

"I'm hoping for your sake that I was right," said Jack. "What do you think you're doing?"

"If she admits that I'm a real Pride-Heart—her Pride-Heart—that's good enough. I think she'll be loyal." She turned to Cricket. "I'm a human, but it's better than me killing you, isn't it?"

Cricket glared at her. "You've managed to control the Heart's Blood. You're giving me magic. You even managed to beat a troll." Her tail flicked back and forth. She looked as though she was thinking. "I suppose I can always take the Heart's Blood when you get yourself killed off on whatever crazy scheme Jack's convinced you of."

Slowly, she lowered her eyes and lay on the ground, tail tucked between her legs and ears flat against her head. Then she rolled over onto her back, exposing a belly and throat covered in soft white fur. This time, Emma did exactly what the Pride-Heart inside her wanted. She placed her hands on Cricket's belly, claws extended, and gently bit the massive cat's throat.

As she pulled back, Cricket shrank, turning into a small ginger cat again, thin and somewhat bloodied. She began to clean herself methodically. "Well, what next?" she said, as if nothing had happened.

Around her, the other cats began to purr softly.

"All right," Emma said. "Before we go, I want to know about that illusion. Helena in the window. What kind of magic is that? It's not cat magic, I know that for sure. I could see it was wrong."

"It looked like faerie magic to me," said Fat Leon, looking at Cricket, "though I didn't have enough magic to see through it at the time."

Cricket nodded. "You're right. A little borrowed faerie enchantment. They didn't like the idea of a human Pride-Heart any more than I did. I told them I'd take care of it."

Jack growled unhappily at this, but his eyes were bright.

"Why don't they like the idea of a human Pride-Heart?" Emma asked.

"Maybe they just don't like humans having magic at all," Cricket said. "Who knows with faeries? I didn't ask. I wanted the Heart's Blood; they wanted a cat to have it instead of a human." She shrugged. "It was a fair swap. I didn't really think you counted as a Pride-Heart, you understand. Now that you do, well, I suppose we can work together. For now."

"So the faeries used Cricket to—what?" She looked at Jack. "Kill me? Why? Why would the faeries want me dead?"

"You're becoming more powerful than you realize," Jack murmured in a self-satisfied tone. "Word gets around."

"We need to go to New Downtown to find out," Emma said. "To 500 Ocean Avenue. Maybe it's a faerie place. Helena loved faeries. She was always reading about them."

Chloe flapped her wings in consternation. "I can't go with you if you're going to New Downtown to find faeries. You're not allowed to fly there if you're a crag. There are laws about it. You have to have a Self-Propelled Sentient Flyer license and a radio and stuff."

Emma thought for a moment. "Well, I guess I could turn you into something—"

"A hawk!" Chloe interrupted.

"—that won't draw as much attention. But something that can still fly."

"I'm not going to become dumb like a hawk, am I?" Chloe asked.

"Um . . ." Emma glanced at Fat Leon.

"You'll have all the intelligence you currently possess," Fat Leon said. "But don't talk too much. And definitely don't scream. It can undo the magic."

Chloe nodded. She seemed excited, too, jerking her wings out as if she might take off at any moment. "Let's do this already. I've never seen New Downtown!"

"Okay, okay," Emma said.

This time, Emma didn't need to struggle to find the magic. It was there, moving through her, out to her cats and back again. Using it was like stretching a limb that had briefly fallen asleep. With the double vision of a human and a cat, she focused on Chloe. If she squinted, Chloe did look like a big hawk, especially when she spread her wings out in excitement like that. You just had to see a beak instead of a face.

There was a soft pop and a rush of air as the space that Chloe had filled suddenly became empty. In its place sat a large hawk. It wobbled a little as it tried to walk, then raised its wings and took off into the air, circling low overhead.

"One more thing," Fat Leon said, with a note of warning in his voice. "Cat magic doesn't work on faeries. Not directly. So you can't just turn one of them into stone the way you can a troll."

Emma nodded. "Jack already told me something like that. Lesson two." She glanced at Jack. "Was there ever going to be a lesson three?"

"Yes. Do what I tell you, and you'll be all right. That's lesson three," Jack said. He purred. "You're going to have to be sneaky and smart with faeries."

"I can do that," Emma said. She felt a little light-headed and dizzy, yet excited at the same time. She was ready for this.

"All right," Jack said. "It's a long walk, so we might as well get started."

They made their way back out of the forest, then followed the tree line for several hours.

It turned out that what the cats thought of as walking was really more of a steady run. Emma found herself tripping and stumbling. Her cats leaped gracefully over obstacles and waited impatiently for her to climb over them.

Finally, Cricket had enough. "Stop clinging to your scrawny human legs," she said. "How are we ever going to get to New Downtown if we have to stop for you every minute?"

Emma looked around at her pride's sleek forms, muscles rippling under their fur. None of them was even breathing hard.

"You know what you need to do," Jack said.

Emma nodded. She did know. Now that she was a Pride-Heart, she should be able to change shape as easily as she changed clothes, and the Heart's Blood wanted her to run with her pride.

She closed her eyes. She imagined herself covered in fur, her muscles sinewy and strong, her furry tail flicking behind her, and felt the sensation of cool water running over her hands and arms like it had when she'd broken free from the ratterking. She dropped to all fours. When she opened her eyes and looked down at herself, she saw tiny paws with wicked-looking claws. Her fur was sleek and black, with a hint of lighter stripes.

She took a step forward, expecting the same clumsiness she'd felt when she'd turned herself into a ratter, but her new shape felt just right. Strong. Fast.

"How do I look?" she asked Jack.

"Like a real Pride-Heart," Jack said, his voice soft. "I knew you could do it."

Emma laughed. "I want to run. Come on!"

She found herself running with ease. The forest seemed to fly by. Her muscles ached pleasantly, her breath was strong, and her heart was quick. With the magic flowing through her and her pride beside her, she felt like she could run forever.

As night fell, they left the forest behind them. They climbed beneath privacy walls, jumped fences, and cut through yards. The buildings became taller, more densely placed. Night gave way to a city's eternal nighttime glow.

They'd entered New Downtown.

# CHAPTER 15

Emma and her pride slunk single file through the city. They stuck to the smaller side streets, trying to avoid the crowds. Most people didn't notice the small, furry creatures darting through the shadows, but those that did crossed the street to avoid them. Chloe soared silently overhead in hawk form.

Cars zoomed past, their lights blindingly bright. Groups of people chattered loudly outside theaters and restaurants. The city seemed a lot bigger and busier when you were a cat.

Emma turned to Cricket. "How much farther to Ocean Avenue?"

"How should I know?" Cricket said. "One of them met me in the forest. I have no idea where they are."

"Then I guess it's up to Chloe to find the place," Emma said.

But that turned out not to be a problem. Chloe was circling around a high-rise with mirrored windows glittering with starlight and city lights. It was many stories taller than any building around it, so tall that the top seemed to disappear into the clouds. And written on the side in projected neon lights was the number 500. This had to be it: 500 Ocean Avenue. The place Helena had been before she disappeared.

Emma hid behind a dumpster. The rest of the pride melted into the shadows, crouching in dark corners or on the fire escapes overhead, slinking along gutters and low roofs. Occasionally their eyes flashed with the reflected light of passing cars.

A line of people wrapped all the way around the building. Most of them looked like teenagers or college students. There were bouncers at the enormous glass doors, deciding who to let in and who to keep waiting outside. It was clearly some kind of nightclub. A faerie one? She remembered Helena sighing over pictures of faerie parties in her magazines, wondering whether she'd ever get to see one.

"This place reeks of faerie magic," Fat Leon whispered with disgust.

"I've never had a Pride-Heart that wanted to hunt faeries

before," Cricket purred. She was tense and her eyes were wide with excitement. "This should be fun."

Chloe circled the building twice, swooping low over the crowd. Then she flew back to Emma, landing a few feet away. She clicked her beak.

"One second," Emma said. She concentrated, felt where reality had shifted to make way for Chloe-the-hawk. She just needed to tweak it a little. The beak, the small dark eyes, the feathers — they shifted, and in their place was Chloe's face, in miniature.

"That's better," Chloe said. She frowned. "I'm squeaky. Why am I squeaky?"

"Well, you're smaller." Emma looked at the line to make sure no one was watching them, but everyone's eyes were fixed on the glittering faerie building. "What did you see?"

"I couldn't see anything inside," Chloe said. "The windows are mirrors all the way up."

"Then we need to get inside ourselves. Chloe, did you see any other doors?"

Chloe shook her head in a quick, birdlike movement. "This is the only entrance. No back door."

Emma's whiskers twitched as she thought. "We could sneak in, but not as cats. There's too many people around. Not as humans, either, since they're only letting certain people in."

"Like we'd turn into humans," Cricket sniffed.

"I don't think you'd be very convincing anyway," Emma said.

"What if you looked like someone who might be inside already?" suggested Jack. "Helena? After all, she was in there at least once. And maybe she never came out. . . ."

Emma stared at him. "You're saying the faeries have Helena?"

Jack shrugged. "It's worth a try. Assuming she's already in there, if they really do have her trapped, they'd let her back in, right?"

"Assuming," said Fat Leon. "But who knows why faeries do anything?"

"Okay," Emma said. "But I want Jack with me. I need a way to get him inside, too."

"What about a huge shiny purse like that girl over there has?" Chloe said, nodding toward a girl clutching a large handbag. "No one would notice him in one of those. If I had a bag like that, I'd fill it up with chocolate, though, not all that makeup and stuff."

"Do you think you could get me one?" Emma said to Chloe. Then she looked down at Jack. "I mean, if you're okay being hidden in a bag."

"Hmm," Jack said. "It's not my first choice, but I'm not letting you go in there alone."

"Good. Then we just need to think of a way to get the rest of you in so you can help." She looked at Chloe again. "Do you think you could cause some kind of a distraction?"

"Do you want me to use my voice?"

Emma winced at the memory of Chloe's harpy screech. "Maybe not. It's no good if we're all falling over in pain. Just . . . once I'm inside, anything you can think of to make them look at you and not at the doors."

"Okay. A distraction and a bag," Chloe said. "I'm on it."

Once Chloe was back in the air, Emma changed the harpy into her normal form. She needed all the magic she had for herself and Jack, and Chloe would be under the police radar flying this low.

Then she took a deep breath and pictured Helena's face, drawing on her memories of her sister, her trendy clothes and streaked hair, the way she walked. Her grin that made you feel like you were both in on some joke. She was the girl who signed Emma's bad report card with their mom's signature. The girl who was always trying to give Emma advice about clothes, but not letting her borrow any of her own.

Helena was the reason Emma was lurking in a dark alley with a pride of impatient cats and a harpy.

Emma let her memories pass through her mind. She felt the running-water magic once again, knew she was changing, just a little. Her skin felt as though it was being stretched, her face was filling out, becoming rounder. Emma opened her eyes and looked down at herself. She was wearing her own clothes—jeans and a T-shirt—but she felt different.

She stepped out of the alley and checked her reflection in the window of the nearest car. Her sister's face stared back at her, a worried crease between her eyes.

Emma's throat felt tight and she reached out to touch the car window. Then she reached up and touched her own face. Helena's face.

"No crying before a hunt," said Jack. "You wouldn't want to disappoint your pride now, would you?"

Emma let her hand fall to her side and turned away from the car. "Yeah, I know," she said. And then she almost did start crying, because the voice that came out of her mouth was so familiar. But Jack was right, she didn't have time for crying. Crying never helped anything.

A large dark shape hit the sidewalk with a soft thump. It was a black purse with a brass leaf clasp and a moon-and-stars logo on one side. Emma waved her thanks to Chloe and picked up the bag. It was empty. Hopefully that meant whoever Chloe had borrowed the bag from still had their things. Maybe she'd stolen it from a store somehow.

"Ready?" she asked Jack, opening the bag for him.

He gave a long-suffering sigh and crawled in. "I hope you know this is all for you." He sniffed. "It smells weird in here."

Emma slung the bag over her shoulder and cut across the street toward the building's entrance. Her heart raced and she wanted to run, but she had to walk steadily, confidently, right to the front of the line. Like she already knew she belonged here and they'd let her in. Like she was under the faeries' spell, just like everyone else here seemed to be.

Two girls sat on bar stools at the glass doors. A bouncer stood behind them, huge arms crossed in front of his chest. They were talking to an older boy who seemed familiar to Emma.

"Come on, I was here last Friday and the dude at the door let me in," the boy was saying. He dug in his pocket and pulled out a phone. "Look, I even took a picture of myself inside, see? That's me right there!"

"Just because you got in on a slow night doesn't mean you can get in today," one of the girls said. "Today's special." She turned to her friend. "What did Corbin call it? Ost . . . Ostara. Something like that." She looked at the boy again. "Everyone wants in. And you can't take photos inside anyway. The faeries have their own exclusive party photographer, even though he can't take pictures of the faeries, either. They just don't show up in the photos at all."

Then Emma realized why the boy seemed so familiar. "Hey, aren't you Marie's brother?" she said.

He glanced at her, annoyed. "What? I mean, yeah. Do I know you?"

"You have to get in line like everyone else," one of the girls said to Emma. Then she started. "Helena? I thought you were inside already. Ooh, that's a great bag! Who is it?"

The second girl looked Emma up and down. "But what *is* that trash you're wearing? I thought you were going to wear that amazing dress Corbin bought you."

Emma's heart was beating fast, and her throat felt tight. *She's really here! She never left this place. Jack was right.*

She swallowed hard and tried to smile at them, but inside she was shaking.

She'd done it. She'd found Helena. She was here with the faeries. Not just an image in a window this time. And she must be all right if these girls expected her to be inside wearing some fancy outfit. Relief and elation battled inside her. She could hardly believe it.

She tried to think of what Helena would say in a situation like this. "I wanted to see if there were any better parties around tonight. No sense in dressing up until you know the place to be!"

The two girls gave her an odd look, but they laughed, so she laughed, as if she'd meant to make a joke.

"You better get changed, the party's already started," the first girl said.

"You have to call it a ball," the other girl whispered. "Corbin doesn't like it when you call it a party."

The girl waved a hand at Emma. "But she just—"

"She's Corbin's favorite, she can do what she wants," the other girl hissed.

"Whatever, they've already started dancing," the first girl said. "Wish I was in there instead of stuck out here with all of this." She waved a hand at Marie's brother and the line of people waiting behind him.

"Hey, so, uh, you think I can go in, too?" Marie's brother asked, trying to win Emma over with the same smile that had failed on the two girls. "Since you know my little sister."

"No way," Emma said. "His sister's a brat and so is he. I don't want him at the party. Ball, I mean." She might not be friends with Marie anymore, but she wasn't about to let her brother disappear the way Helena had. Not now that she knew the faeries had something to do with it.

"Whatever," one of the girls said. She dismissed Marie's brother with another wave of her hand. His face turned red and Emma thought he was going to argue, but one look from the bouncer and he turned away.

"Thanks," Emma said. "I'm going inside now. I'll talk to you later. Bye!"

She brushed past them quickly.

Behind her, she heard shouts and then Chloe's voice.

"Who're you calling a pigeon? You're the ones waddling around in those funny shoes, squawking at each other!"

There was her distraction.

Emma didn't stop to listen. A set of sliding glass doors opened for her, leading into a wide, carpeted hall lit with candles. An orange streak shot past her legs, almost tripping her. She caught a hint of Cricket's scent just as the cat turned down a hallway. She hoped the other cats had managed to get in, too.

"Hey! What was that?" the bouncer cried out, peering down the hallway. He spotted Emma. "Oh, Lady Helena—I thought I saw something run in here. Did you see where it went?"

"I didn't see anything," Emma lied.

The bouncer nodded. "Well, if you see anything, let someone from security know. No need to bother the lords and ladies if it's just a squirrel. I've got bigger problems right now with that harpy outside anyway. Do you think it got out of the zoo? I'll have someone check. They need locks on those things, I don't care what anyone says."

*They have a zoo? Here?* Emma thought. And then: *Lady Helena?*

But all she said was, "Yeah, you're right." Helena would know about a zoo. She had to keep a straight face.

As she walked away, the glass doors swished closed behind her, dulling the sound of people and traffic outside. Now Emma could hear the thump of bass somewhere ahead of her.

Jack poked his head out of the handbag, his one eye sparkling. He was in a good mood. "Not bad. You're a pretty good liar, for a human. The cat part of you is clearly taking over."

"Lie down," Emma whispered. "We're getting near the main

room now." She felt him settle and begin to purr at the bottom of the bag.

At the end of the hall were two arched wooden doors, open wide, and beyond them a huge room, filled with people talking and laughing and dancing, and dressed in clothes that were probably worth more than everything Emma owned. The floral scent of perfume choked her. It was obviously the ballroom. And somewhere in there was Helena.

"I think I'm underdressed," she muttered into the bag.

"Why didn't you think of that when you turned yourself into your sister?" Jack demanded. She could see his ears twitching inside the bag.

"I just didn't, okay? Besides, it's hard to imagine a dress on the spot."

She scanned the hallway until she found a sign for bathrooms, and ducked in. Several girls stood in front of the half-size mirror above the sinks, applying makeup and making minute adjustments to their hair and dresses. Emma quickly went into the closest stall. She'd changed herself into a cat, right? This couldn't be that hard.

"I'm going to give myself a purple dress like one of the girls by the mirror," she whispered. Emma had never been very interested in clothes, so it was hard to imagine a dress in enough detail to make it look decent, or to know what it felt like or how it moved. She closed her eyes, felt the coolness of running water once more.

She waited until the other girls had left and the bathroom was empty. Then she checked herself out in a mirror. It looked like two dresses—one purple and one black, with completely different cuts—had been smashed together.

"How does it look?" she asked Jack.

"How should I know?" Jack said. "Only humans and faeries care about dresses."

"I'm sure it's good enough," Emma said, though she felt a little worried. "It's dark in there anyway, right? Maybe they won't notice." She looked at herself critically. The purple and black actually managed to look kind of cool, or so she hoped. "It's fine," she told him. "As long as I'm not wearing jeans."

She went back out into the hallway leading to the ballroom. There was a press of people all pushing to get in now, and she soon found herself swept along with them into the ballroom itself.

The noise was deafening. People chattered and yelled and shouted, and four different DJs were spinning different songs on four different dance floors. Dim, hooded lights were set in the floor but the room was lit from above by a massive lamp made to look like the moon and which cast everything in pale blue light. There were stars, too—thousands of blue lights twinkling cold and bright all over the ceiling. Emma had never seen so many stars before, not even on the clearest winter night. For a moment she felt as though she were out in the desert, all alone beneath the sky with no city lights to dull their beauty.

Then she shook her head. She was a cat, not just a human. She could see through faerie magic. *It's all fake,* she told herself. *Just like those twigs at the Red Caboose.*

Emma scanned the ballroom carefully. She thought she caught a glimpse of something orange stalking through the shadows against one wall, and another cat shadow as it darted up a speaker system that was taller than she was.

"Looks like at least some of the pride got in," she whispered into the bag, though with the noise level, her whisper was really more of a shout. If Jack answered her, she couldn't hear it.

Emma pushed through the crowd, toward the center of the ballroom. That was where the crowd seemed to be packed the tightest. She had to use her claws once or twice—just little jabs, that was all—to squeeze in closer and see what was going on. She hoped Jack didn't accidentally get squished. She felt the bag wriggle.

Finally, the people wouldn't move even when she scratched them. They stood, squeezed together and gazing up with delight. Emma followed their gaze . . . and saw the faeries.

# CHAPTER 16

The faeries sat on a wide, six-foot-high platform in the center of the main ballroom. It was the same circular stage Emma had seen in the ratterking's mind. Only this time it wasn't empty. Eight faeries, male and female, lounged on cushioned chairs. They were beautiful.

Most of them were tall and thin. But that wasn't what made them beautiful. It was their perfect skin: Some were so pale they seemed to glow with moonlight, while others were a rich shining bronze, and a few almost as dark as the shadows. It was the way they moved, graceful and powerful even when they were merely dangling their legs over the sides of their chairs. It was their voices, clear and musical, cutting through the noise of the ballroom, each word more melodious, each phrase more harmonious, than any song Emma had ever heard.

A part of Emma wanted to talk to them, to look at them, to be around them for no other reason than that their presence seemed to fill the room with magic.

But at the same time, like a hazy double vision, like the sunlight on the window of the Red Caboose, she saw something else. Something not at all human. She stared, the realization creeping up on her. Cat magic could see through faerie magic — and it meant she could see through the faeries themselves. Their faeries' beauty was a disguise. A veil of glamour. Their true forms were different. So different.

Underneath the veil of glamour, they were oddly proportioned. One was only a few feet tall, with a stick-thin body and a large, round head. Instead of hair, long willow leaves hung down in front of its face, and its skin was dark and rough like bark. Another seemed to be little more than a pile of leaves and ivy until it moved, walking on legs made of twigs and gesturing with hands of rosebuds and thorns.

Most disturbing of all, none of them had eyes. They had hands and legs, and seemed to have mouths — or must, somewhere under all the leaves and vines, or else how could they talk? A few even had noses, or gnarly things that looked like noses. But Emma couldn't see a single set of eyes.

*Faeries can make some people see what they want*, Jack had said. *They make themselves look beautiful, sound beautiful, smell beautiful. So of course humans fall in love with them.*

She couldn't read their faces, couldn't guess what such creatures might be thinking. There was something otherworldly about them, stranger than any crag she'd encountered before. And yet she found that even without their disguise she didn't want to look away. She watched them for a minute, as if mesmerized. It seemed that the longer she stared at any one of them, the more she saw. Small flowers bloomed among the vines even as she watched, petals falling unnoticed to the floor, only to bloom again. A spider spun a web between the twig-faerie's ears, round and round without ever seeming to finish.

She felt she could lose herself watching them. The thought sent a shiver up her spine, and in that moment she pulled her gaze away. It was only the human part of her that was drawn to the faeries, she realized. The cat part could see through it all. She had to remember that.

She was a Pride-Heart with true cat magic, while all the faeries had were tricks and illusions. She could do this.

Emma tried to get closer, but there were guards around the

platform keeping the crowd back. People yelled and shoved, trying to catch the faeries' attention.

"I saw you in the park the other day. You smiled at me! Would you dance with me?"

"Ever since I heard you sing it's all I can think about. I can't listen to music, can't play my guitar—none of it sounds right!"

"I sent you another poem! Did you have time to read it? Do you want me to read it to you now? I brought a copy just in case."

"How about a contest?" the faerie with the spiderweb said. Her glamour disguise was a ghostly pale girl in a dress that glowed like moonlight. She laid her head in the arms of a wide-eyed human girl. "Don't stare at me," the faerie said softly to the girl. Even with all the noise it was impossible not to hear her. "You know you mustn't." The girl nodded quickly and looked away from the faerie, scanning the crowd slowly instead, meeting people's eyes for a moment before moving on.

*They're using humans to see*, Emma realized with a start. That was why they had humans with them on the stage. *They're looking through their eyes.* Did the humans know they were being used like some kind of eye-puppets? Would they even care if they did?

One of the other faeries laughed. He seemed to be made of evergreens and honeysuckle and ivy. His glamour disguise, a dark-skinned man in black leather pants and a ruffled shirt unbuttoned to his chest, rolled its eyes. "You only want a contest because you always win. But all right. It's a day of change, after all. But it must be someone new, not one of your usual admirers." He turned his head toward the eager faces just beyond the platform, and made his choice. "You, boy with the black hair and silver shirt. Would you like to play a game with us?" he asked, though there was no doubt what the answer would be. "Let him through."

The crowd reluctantly parted to allow an older boy through. He stared, bewildered, at the faeries. The spiderweb faerie motioned for him to come closer, and he did, though the guards didn't let him up onto the platform itself.

"The game is very simple," the spiderweb faerie explained. "You must pick which one of us you prefer. Me?"

"Or me?" the honeysuckle faerie said.

"This is boring," the faerie with the willow-leaf hair complained, though even complaining her voice sounded like wind chimes and soft woodwind pipes. "Do I have to sit here and watch these two show off?" She spoke to the human next to her, a girl in a long ruffled skirt and glasses.

"Well, have you decided?" the spiderweb faerie said, her glamour grinning mischievously.

"I pick you, of course," the boy said, his voice hoarse.

"Are you sure?" the honeysuckle faerie said, a teasing sort of pout in his voice.

"No! No, of course not," the boy said as soon as he looked over at the other faerie. "I only have eyes for you."

"What a perfect phrase," the spiderweb faerie whispered. "It makes me sad to hear you say so to another."

"I'm sorry! I don't know why I said it. I was a fool, I—"

Emma realized the boy had tears running down his face, and a sheen of sweat made his forehead glisten. She wondered if she should do something, if she could help him somehow. It was like watching one of her own cats playing with some small rodent they happened to find.

"Helena?" said the willow-leaf faerie then.

Her human companion with the glasses was staring right at Emma.

"What are you doing down there?" said the faerie. "And where did you get that dress? Has Corbin seen it yet? I can't wait to see his face when he finds out you didn't wear the one he got you." The girl with the glasses nodded slightly, as if this had been an order. "Join us! This is your special day. You should see and be seen—and enjoy it all while you can."

Emma started to shake her head, then realized that would be a mistake. No one here would ever refuse a faerie request. Maybe she'd have been better off disguised as no one in particular and just waiting for Helena to show up. But she wouldn't have got into the place then. Anyway, it was too late now.

"Come on, you're almost family now," the willow-leaf faerie said. "You're allowed to sit with us even if Corbin is taking forever. Let her through, please!"

"Nissa, hush," the spiderweb faerie said, before turning back to her game.

So Emma found herself pushed out of the crowd, past the miserable boy still trying to decide which faerie he preferred, past the guards, and up the short spiral stairs to the platform. She clutched the handbag close to her side.

"Are you okay in there?" she hissed into it.

"I would be if you'd stop squashing me," Jack said. "What's going on? I can hear that faerie. Be careful."

She didn't have time to reply. Two of the human girls on the platform stole quick glances at her as she walked past.

"I heard Corbin's in love with her, and that's why he's taking her to the twenty-seventh floor," one of them whispered.

"I wish Corbin was in love with me," one of the girls sighed. "She hasn't even been here that long, it's not fair. What does she have that I don't?"

"Maybe she's not as lucky as you think. I've heard stories about the twenty-seventh floor. Jen says that there's a way into the Deep Forest from it, and that they do all sorts of magic there, magic no one's supposed to know about."

The Deep Forest? Emma had never heard anyone refer to Old

Downtown that way. But maybe she was talking about something else, some kind of faerie place.

"Well, if no one's supposed to know about it, how does Jen know?" the other girl whispered. "She's such a liar."

"You weren't here this time last year. It's always the same day. High Spring, of course. Or Ostara, or whatever they call it. Hilary went up, and Liz and Greg. Where are they now?"

"How should I know? I'm not them. They get bored with people, you know they do. Sometimes I worry Miv is getting bored with me . . . I don't even think he's looking through me right now." She gazed longingly at the dark-skinned faerie.

"Come, sit here," the willow-leaf faerie called Nissa said, motioning at Emma with hands of reed and bramble while her beautiful illusory self waved elegantly at a spot on the floor beside her.

Emma sat, not sure what was expected of her, and balanced Jack-in-the-bag on her knees. Did Helena stay quiet like all the other humans here? She had a hard time believing that. Helena had never been one to sit quiet for anything.

"So how are you feeling?" Nissa said. "Not frightened, I hope? There's nothing to be frightened of, you'll do just fine."

"I'm sure it'll be great," Emma said nervously. The girl with the glasses was staring at her intently.

Nissa leaned closer and grinned. Not with the version of herself

Emma was supposed to see, but with her real mouth, a mouth filled with glistening rose thorns.

Emma recoiled. She couldn't help it.

The girl with the glasses frowned, but the faerie only grinned wider.

"I knew there was something wrong with you!" Nissa hissed, and the sound was like a distant waterfall. "You can see me, can't you? I thought I felt something strange about you. Ha! Just wait until Corbin finds out . . . oh, this is going to be fun, I think."

Emma felt Jack shift in the handbag, felt his low growl.

"Can you see the others, too?" Nissa whispered. "You can, can't you?" She chuckled through her thorny teeth. "Corbin always gets the best toys. He'll never appreciate you the way I would. I'd never try to turn you at all, oh no! What a waste of wonderful, wondrous eyes!"

Emma wasn't sure what the faerie was talking about, but none of it sounded very good, for herself or for Helena. The faeries treated Helena like a toy? And turn her into what? But she couldn't ask, because the real Helena would already know. She stood. "I really should go find Corbin, I think. Maybe someone can take me to him?"

"No. I want you to stay," Nissa said. "You won't be any good after tonight, so I'll have to borrow your eyes until then."

The girl with the glasses glanced at the faerie. "Lady Nissa, you know Lord Corbin hates it when you—"

"Hush," Nissa said. "This is too good a chance to pass up. He's the one that's let her wander around on her own, after all."

The girl stopped talking, though her mouth tightened and her eyes narrowed with jealousy as she stared at Emma.

But Emma forgot about her a moment later as an itching sensation began building at the back of her eyes. For a second the room seemed to brighten, everything glowing with light and color. It was like she'd been plunged into the faeries' magic, surrounded by it and filled with it.

Nissa was using her eyes, disrupting her cat magic.

She hissed, and then her claws were out. Instantly, the itching sensation disappeared and the room no longer glowed. Her stomach dropped to the floor as she realized Helena's appearance had melted away, along with her black-and-purple dress. She was Emma once more, dressed in her old jeans and T-shirt.

Behind her glasses, the human girl's eyes widened.

"She's that cat! Corbin warned us about her!" Nissa cried out, her voice a mix of fear and excitement.

All around her the faeries started, but there was a moment's pause before their human eye-puppets thought to turn and look at her. It was the only moment Emma was going to get. She grabbed the handbag, ran up to the edge of the platform, and jumped onto the railing. At least that's what she'd meant to do. But something snatched at her ankle as she jumped, breaking her momentum. She fell hard, and her stomach slammed into the railing.

The bag flew from her arm, spilling Jack onto the floor amid the crowd.

Hanging there, half off the platform, Emma could see all the way to the other end of the club. Time seemed to slow as a door opened and a couple stepped out.

A faerie, short and round like a toad. He had green-brown skin. Moss covered the top of his head, and tendrils of what looked like seaweed hung in a long mustache from his face. Where Emma thought his eyes should be were lily pads. And beside him stood a girl in a dress that sparkled red and blue. She had streaked hair and a quick smile. An easy, unstoppable walk.

Helena.

Emma tried to shout her sister's name, but she had no breath. Instead, she watched, unable to move. But Jack had seen Helena, too, had recognized her from the illusion at the Red Caboose. He darted through the crowd toward her.

Nissa's girl was gazing after him. The faerie mustn't realize what Jack was doing. Emma had to use her magic. For an instant she panicked. Then a fly flew past her nose and she knew what to do. She focused on the girl, just like she had with the troll. She saw the nightclub with her cat-human double vision. She reached out for the girl as if she were right beside her. And then it was done.

Nissa and the girl in glasses screamed, and the girl fell back onto the platform, covering her eyes with her arm. "My eyes! There's something wrong with my eyes!" she shrieked.

Emma had given her the eyes of a fly, eyes that showed a thousand different versions of the scene around them. They would take a while to get used to, Emma thought. She'd change them back later, but right now she didn't have time for sympathy. She had to be like a cat.

Emma pushed herself off the platform, forcing herself to breathe as she hit the floor on all fours, crouching.

Behind and above her, the faeries began shouting, and she heard Nissa's voice. "That girl, the one with the claws! A cat-girl! She's dangerous to all faeries. If you ever loved us, you'll bring her to me!"

Emma retracted her claws as people turned to her. The two guards that had been standing at the platform each drew thin green wands from their belts and started toward her, pushing aside anyone that got in their way. A man in a biker's jacket pushed back, and one of the wands shot out, smacking him in the head. The man crumpled to the ground, twitching. Wisps of blue smoke poured out of his nose and ears.

They were coming for her, and if they got her, she would lose Helena forever.

Then Emma felt a tugging inside her and the pull of magic

from all around her. The pride. Her cats were here and they wanted magic. She gave them what they needed.

Deep, chest-rumbling roars exploded from all around the club. The music was cut off entirely, and then the only other sounds were shouts and screams as huge cats leaped among the crowd. They batted people aside with their giant paws, eyes shining in the nightclub lights.

"Be careful! Don't hurt anyone!" Emma shouted. Everywhere people were running, yelling, screaming. At this rate someone was going to get trampled. But she had to keep going, had to try and find Helena while she still had a chance.

Before she could do anything she felt strong hands grip her shoulder, spinning her around. Then there was a flash of golden fur and Cricket had one of the hands in her mouth and was shaking the guard attached to it back and forth. She was going to kill him.

"Stop it!" Emma yelled. "He's just doing what they told him. He can't help it!"

Cricket dropped the man and looked up at Emma. Blood flecked the white fur around her mouth. "But this is a hunt," she said. "If no one gets hurt, what's the point?"

Emma hesitated, not sure what to say, and in that moment the second guard lunged forward, jabbing at Cricket's neck with her thin green wand. Cricket twitched and yowled pitifully, shrinking down to a ginger cat again, her eyes rolling up to the back of her head. Emma started forward. Without thinking she slashed viciously at the guard. The guard cried out, clutching her arm to her chest. Cricket lay still and smoking, but she was alive. Emma picked her up by the scruff of her neck and ran.

She found the Toe-Chewer a few yards away. He had feathers and a pair of enormous wings, which he was flapping frantically.

"I'm a harpy!" he yelled. "Isn't it great?"

"You have to get Cricket out of here," Emma cried. "Then find the others, tell them to run—and not to hurt anyone else!"

"But we're supposed to protect you," he said.

"You're supposed to do what I say," Emma snapped.

The Toe-Chewer nodded at Cricket. "Is she supposed to be smoking like that?"

"She'll be fine," Emma said. "I hope. Now get out of here! I have to find Helena!"

The Tow-Chewer held Cricket in his mouth and waddled through the ballroom, bashing the screaming crowd as he went. Emma could see the other cats starting to follow. She turned and ran toward the door where she'd seen Helena and Jack. But when she reached it, neither of them was there.

Emma stared around, feeling suddenly hopeless and angry. What had she been expecting? For Helena and that faerie to wait around while huge cats rampaged through the club? He probably took Helena away as soon as the screaming started. If that had been Helena at all. Emma couldn't help doubting herself now, doubting everything she'd done. It had all gone wrong, and a part of her wanted to turn back, to stay with her pride.

Whatever choice she made, it felt like she was abandoning someone.

Then Jack appeared at the door. "Are you coming or not?" he called. "She went this way. Hurry!"

# CHAPTER 17

Emma burst through the door and ran down the hallway, with Jack a little in front of her, leading the way. There were a few people in the hall, but no sign of either Helena or the toad faerie. Was that faerie Corbin? Was he using Helena as his own eye-puppet?

Emma felt sick at the thought, but didn't stop running. "Where did they go?" she yelled to Jack.

"I only saw her for a minute," Jack said. "She was with a faerie and—"

"He took her somewhere, I know it," Emma interrupted.

"Do you want to hear what they said or not?"

"Sorry."

"That's better," Jack said. "He told her the ceremony was going to take a few hours. That they didn't have much time to spend here, but he wanted to see it all with her one last time."

"That other faerie, Nissa, she said something like that, too," Emma said. "When she thought I was Helena, she said soon it would be too late to see through my eyes and I was family, and something about Corbin turning me." Emma stopped. "It almost sounds like—"

"Like they're going to turn your sister into one of them?"

Emma nodded. "But how can they? I thought only cat magic could actually change things. That faerie magic was just an illusion."

"Maybe they're using some other kind of magic," Jack said. "If there's enough of it in the Deep Forest to overrun a city, maybe there's enough to turn a human into a faerie."

Emma caught her breath. "I heard one of the girls on the platform say something about the twenty-seventh floor, that there's a way into the Deep Forest from it. That might be where they went. Help me look for an elevator!"

Emma and Jack darted around corners, but there were no signs anywhere. If you were here, you were supposed to know where you were going.

She slowed, listening carefully. She heard the distant chaos from the ballroom. Then the faint *ding* of an elevator and the scraping of metal as a set of doors slid open.

"This way!" Emma cried, then turned and ran down the hallway toward the sound. There it was, an elevator. Empty. The doors started to close and Emma flung out her arm to stop them, slipping into the compartment with Jack hot on her heels.

Inside there was a panel of numbered buttons. They went from one to twenty-six, but there was no twenty-seven.

"What now?" she asked Jack.

"Now you think of something sneaky and smart," Jack said.

Emma stared at the buttons a moment longer, then reached out and pressed twenty-six. "Maybe I can find some stairs at the top," she said, but without much confidence. They probably didn't want just anyone strolling right into the middle of their secret ceremony. Still, there had to be a way to get there.

The button flashed at her and the elevator started moving. Emma watched the digital display change as they passed each floor.

4 . . . 5 . . . 6 . . .

"If we do find her," Emma said, hesitating, "how am I supposed to get her out again? How are *we* getting out again?"

10 . . . 11 . . . 12 . . .

"With difficulty," Jack said. "And magic."

"Thanks. You're a ton of help."

16 . . . 17 . . . 18 . . .

"This might be a good time for lesson four," Jack said. "Remember how I said cat magic doesn't work on faeries?"

"Yeah."

"That might only be true for actual cats. For a human Pride-Heart . . . well, that's different."

21 . . . 22 . . . 23 . . .

"What? Why didn't you tell me before?" Emma said.

"You weren't ready," Jack said. He glanced up at her. "You're probably not ready now. But it sounds like your sister's out of time, so you need to use whatever you've got."

The elevator dinged, and the doors swung open. Jack leaped out, and Emma followed.

The twenty-sixth floor turned out to be the zoo the bouncer had mentioned. Emma stopped and stared. Paths wound their way between floor-to-ceiling Plexiglas cages. Small trees and bushes were set into pots along the path, and somewhere Emma heard the sound of running water.

But the animals inside the cages weren't animals at all. They were crags. She saw five ratters with their tails tied together. They sniffed at her as she walked past, and chattered excitedly. There was a troll sitting among a bunch of rocks and bushes, so still she wasn't sure he was actually alive until he turned his head to follow her with his stony eyes. A large gray wolf paced back and forth, and a lone dwarf reclined in a hammock, counting gold coins. Two merfolk floated in a small pool.

Jack padded beside her, his tail bristling.

"Should we help them?" Emma said.

"And how do you think you can do that?" Jack asked impatiently.

"We can let them out at least."

Jack spat. "You think they're locked in? The only thing keeping them here is their love for faeries, or gold, or whatever it is the faeries make them see. These crags are just as tied to faeries as humans. The faeries don't need locks. Their pets are happy to stay in their cages. Come on, before someone finds us. Look, there's a door."

In front of them was a narrow door with a crescent moon painted on it. Emma threw the door open and found herself looking into a small stairwell—with stairs leading up.

She dashed through the door and took the stairs two at a time.

At the top there was another door. She turned the knob without bothering to slow down, slamming the door open with her shoulder—and tumbling out into an open space. The night sky glowed above her and she could see the lights of the city spread all around, blotted out by the darkness of the forest in the distance.

They were on the roof of the high-rise. There was no twenty-seventh floor.

And in front of them stood Nissa and the girl with insect eyes.

"Hello, little cat," said the faerie. "I wondered how long it would take you to get here. I wanted to thank you for the improvements you made to Jen. She had interesting eyes before, but now they're absolutely fabulous. What other kinds of eyes could you make for Nissa if you stayed here? Since you're not Helena after all, Corbin can't complain if I keep you for myself."

The door behind Emma slammed shut. Emma spun around and pulled on the handle, but it wouldn't move. Her heart sank.

Jack hissed and spat. "She's *my* Pride-Heart, faerie. And you're going to tell us where to find Helena and the ceremony."

"*Tsk, tsk,*" Nissa said. "Little cats aren't supposed to know about such things."

Emma looked at the girl. "I'm sorry about your eyes. I'll fix them. I just needed to get away."

"No!" Jen said. Her hands flew to her face, as though she was shielding herself from Emma. "No, please don't. I want to keep them."

"But if I don't, you'll be stuck like that forever. You can't really want to live like that for the rest of your life. It's crazy!"

"You don't understand," Jen said. "I want Lady Nissa to be happy." She glanced at the faerie and smiled, then fixed her eyes on Emma again just as quickly.

Nissa bared her thorn-teeth at Emma. "I'd rather you didn't ruin her, cat-girl. Unless, of course, you want to take her place . . ."

"You heard Jack," said Emma to the faerie. "Where's Helena?"

"Oh, no." Nissa shook her head. "I can't tell you that, I'm afraid. You're going to have to miss the ceremony. I wanted to make sure I found you first. But everyone's looking for you. They'll put you in a nice cage. Or maybe they'll just have you quietly killed. Such a waste! Stay with Nissa. Let Nissa have your eyes. Let yourself love Nissa like a sister. Better than a sister. You can turn yourself into so many wondrous creatures. Bird, fish, cat. You can give me so many ways to see the world."

"If she's not going to tell you anything, turn her into a mouse," Jack spat. "Then we can throw her off the roof, or leave her for the others to find. Maybe they'll put her in a nice cage, too."

Nissa laughed. "You know cats can't change faeries. That's a law almost as old as the forests."

"Oh, you're right, of course," Jack purred, his eye half closed. "But she's a Pride-Heart and a human, too. I don't think the same rules apply to her."

Nissa turned back to Emma. "Corbin told us there was a human Pride-Heart. He's afraid of you, but the others are too wrapped up in their own games to care much," she said. "But you don't want to fight, do you? I see that in you, cat-girl. Stay with Nissa. You'll be Nissa's favorite."

Emma saw Jen flinch at that, though the girl didn't take her creepy eyes off Emma. Who was she? Emma wondered. She didn't look much older than Helena. Did she have a family out there somewhere, looking for her? What would they think to see her now, begging Emma not to take away her insect eyes?

"Jen, you don't have to stay here," she said. "Come back with me. After I find my sister, I'll help you get home."

"I don't want to! I'm happy here!" Jen screamed, her eyes filling with tears.

Emma stepped toward her, and took her by the arm. "You don't have to do what she says."

Jen screamed again, and only then did Emma really focus on the girl's face — twisted up with fear and loss and hatred. Too late.

Before Emma could react, Jen barreled into her, crying and hitting and pushing her back — until suddenly there was no more roof under Emma's feet, and she fell from the high-rise, too surprised even to yell out.

# CHAPTER 18

Emma opened her eyes to darkness. She was lying flat on her back, staring up at the night sky. Wet grass brushed her neck, and something small and furry was sitting on her stomach. Emma lifted her head and saw the Toe-Chewer staring back at her, his big bright eyes glinting in the dark.

More cats weighed down her legs, and Cricket was curled up under her arm, her tail tickling Emma's nose. She sat up, pushing them all away.

"What happened? Where am I?"

"In the trailer park," the Toe-Chewer said. "Chloe saw you fall off the roof. She saved you. Good thing you'd turned her back into a harpy before you went into the club. Good thing your parents aren't here, too."

The last thing Emma remembered was falling, after she and Jack had—

"Where's Jack?" she said. She looked around, trying to spot his white fur.

"Recovering from what your giant chicken did to me," Jack said from behind her. "I tried to tell her that we should stay there, that we needed to find a way back in, but she wouldn't listen! And now we're running out of time!"

"Next time I'll leave you on the roof, then," Chloe called from her perch on the trailer roof. "Anyway, you wouldn't have gotten pinched if you hadn't moved so much. My instincts kick in when small, furry animals are squirming in my talons, all yummy and delicious."

"Thank you," Emma told Chloe. "For saving me and Jack." Her shoulders were aching, probably from where Chloe had dug in her talons to fly her to safety. She must have passed out.

"Everyone needs a harpy on their team," replied Chloe, but she looked pleased. "It's been a long night. I'm going to grab a nap." She tucked her head under one of her wings.

"We have to go back in there and find the twenty-seventh

floor," Jack said. "I might have found it if she hadn't swooped in!"

"I don't think we'll find it that way," Emma said. She rubbed her eyes, trying to think. "We have to get to Helena before they turn her into a faerie. There might be others, too." She stopped, remembering. "Those girls at the club said something about the twenty-seventh floor connecting to the Deep Forest, but that doesn't make any sense? New Downtown is nowhere near the forest, or Old Downtown."

"The Deep Forest isn't the same as Old Downtown," Jack said. "It's somewhere else. The forest over Old Downtown can take you there, if you know where to look, but the Deep Forest goes to other places, too."

"Is it still a forest, though?" Emma asked. "Some kind of super-extra-magical hidden forest that leads right to Helena?"

"Something like that," Jack said.

"We don't go there," Cricket said. "Nothing to hunt. And it's easy to get lost."

"It can't be that bad," Emma said. "Can it? Isn't there some kind of magical forest map we could use or something?"

The cats stared at her in that way they had, which said that no matter how much magic she could do, she was still a really strange Pride-Heart.

"So the little cat returns," a too-sweet voice said from behind her.

Emma turned. The hag was peering at her over the fence separating the two trailers.

"They were looking for you last night. Mommy calling the police, yelling at trees, waking harmless old ladies from their dreams and making accusations. I told them I wouldn't eat cat even if I had my teeth." She smacked her lips. "The woman's crying reminds me of older times, ah, when my belly was still full. They left with police."

Emma flinched and walked to the fence. "I didn't mean to worry them. But I found my sister. I was trying to get her back."

"Playing with faeries, eh?" the hag said, smiling her toothless smile. "It's a wonder you came back at all. They hunts in packs instead of all alone like hags, but not so different. Both needs childrens, only faeries wastes them on stupid things."

"What do you mean? Why do they need children?"

The hag laughed. "Yes, clever faeries. They likes to live near humans, near human childrens."

"At least they don't eat anyone," Emma said.

"That they don't," the hag said sadly. "They turns them into little wisps of dream instead of nice, soft meats. So thin a tiny breeze could blow them all away. Maybe soon hags will be like that, too. All the skin and bones melting away until only shadows is left."

"You've seen them turning children into faeries?"

"Long ago," the hag said. "When I still had my teeth. Hiding in the Deep Forest, trying to forget my aching belly. No hiding from it now." The hag sighed heavily.

"But that means you know how to get to them! To the ceremony."

"Yes," she nodded. "Hags can walk through the dark places. Forest is bigger than it looks, and has deep roots."

Emma tried to stay calm, but her hopes were already rising. "Take me there. I have to find my sister before it's too late, before she turns into one of those things."

"Ha! And why would a hag do something like that?" the hag said. "The Deep Forest is dangerous. There is more there than poor hags."

"I have power," Emma said. "I'll protect you."

"And who will protect you?" the hag said, chuckling. "Even cats fear the Deep Forest, as do any who can feel afraid."

"Please," Emma said. "If you know the way to the faeries, help me."

The hag shuffled back and forth, muttering to herself for several moments. She tapped her long fingernails against her trailer. Then she turned back to Emma, a strange gleam in her eyes. "Yes, yes, will takes little cat to Deep Forest and will sniffs out your sister, but you must finds your way back out again."

"So you'll do it?" Emma asked. Getting there in time was the important thing right now. Once she found Helena, she'd figure out how to get home.

"Hags not meant to waste away in little metal boxes," the hag said. "Hags belong in the Deep Forest. Starving here, and still hunted. But not so helpless as they all thinks. Wait on that side. Don't crush my mushrooms."

The hag hunched down and dug in the dirt at the back corner of her yard. She dug until Emma heard her fingernails clink against glass, then she pulled out a dingy-looking bottle with a stopper. Clutching it to her chest, she hobbled back toward Emma.

"What's that?" Emma asked.

The hag grinned. "Hags is sneaky, too. I hids it before they came to tear out the rest. The smallest one." Then she opened the bottle and tipped it over her hand, shaking it gently. A small, white object fell into her palm. It looked like a shark's tooth. The hag picked it up and held it against her gums. There was a soft sucking sound and the tooth disappeared into the hag's mouth. "Now, what will I have to taste? Have you brought a nice little finger bone for me to suck the marrow from?"

Emma stared openmouthed at the hag. "You mean one of Helena's? No, of course not! Why would you even think something like that?"

"Needs to have something to start with. I can finds faeries, but if you wants your sister I needs a taste, a smell, the sound of little tears. Too much distance. Too many lost little childrens. Hard to find just one."

"I could bring you a photograph. And some of her clothes might still smell."

The hag chuckled to herself. "I taste and smell and hear, but not like a cat. Nothing like a cat. Needs a part of her. Bones is best, but flesh and blood will do. Have you brought me some of that? Yes, yes, of course you have. A little treat for a poor old woman."

"You can't have one of my fingers, if that's what you mean," Emma said. "I'm still using them all."

"Not all of them. Not the little ones," the hag said, smacking her lips together. Then she scowled. "But no, the cat will be all in your bones now, settling in and making them bitter. But a little bite should do the trick. Easy enough to tell you and sister apart now that you smell of cat."

"I don't trust her," Jack said, from behind Emma. "You don't need her kind of magic."

"It's fine. We made a bargain and everything. Bargains between crags are always magic in the movies: You can't break them." She tried to sound flippant, but knew she wasn't really pulling it off. She raised her voice. "Besides, I'll have my pride with me in case she tries anything."

As if on cue, Emma's pride came forward to surround her in a protective semicircle.

"The Heart-Killer's right," Fat Leon said. "A hag's kind of magic doesn't help anyone but her."

"And hunters do their own hunting," added Cricket, her tail flicking from side to side.

But Emma held out her arm. It was the only way to find Helena in time. "Just a small bite and that's it. Will it, um, hurt much?" She immediately felt stupid for saying it. She was supposed to be a Pride-Heart now. She had to be braver than that.

The hag's fingers twitched as if to grab Emma, but she hesitated, glaring at the cats. "Yes, yes, a little bite, that's all," she whispered.

"Do it, then," Emma said.

The hag grinned and wrapped one hand around Emma's wrist, and her mouth opened. And then Emma saw her shadow move. It was too dark and solid to be cast by moonlight, too real. The shadow opened its mouth, wider and wider, wide enough to swallow Emma whole. The hairs on the back of her neck stood on end. She wanted her claws, wanted to fight. Was this what it was like for the children the hag had eaten? Her cats hissed and spat, and Emma felt her palms tingle. *You made a deal*, she told herself. *And it's Helena's last chance.*

The shadow's mouth closed over her arm just below the elbow. There was a sharp pain, and a numbness, like she'd been stung by a wasp. Then the shadow melted away.

The hag made a face like she'd just bitten into something rotten. "Not so sweet now. Not so sweet at all. But maybe for the best, maybe not so good to taste and not feel full."

"Can you find her? My sister?" Emma asked anxiously, rubbing her elbow. There was a bright red mark where the skin had been pierced.

"Maybe, maybe. If this little cat can get past howlers, not much farther to faeries. I sniffs out your sister then we parts ways, yes?"

"Yes," Jack said. "We have to go now, before we're too late."

Emma's pride looked tense, excited. Their tails swished back and forth, and their eyes were shining.

"I'll wait here for you," said Chloe, raising her head from her wing. "If your parents come back, I'll tell them you were here."

"You aren't coming?" Emma asked.

"Can't," the harpy sighed. "Even I'm not stupid enough to fly in the Deep Forest, and someone has to make sure your parents don't go charging after you. That's the sort of thing human parents do, right? Like in that episode about the kidnapped twins and the evil robots from the opposite dimension. But you have to tell me everything that happened when you get back. I'm sure you'll make it. You have some crazy luck!"

Emma nodded. "I'll be back. Don't worry about me. Tell my parents not to worry, either, okay?"

Chloe put her head back under her wing. Loud snores began to shake the trailer.

Then Emma and her pride followed the hag into the forest.

*　*　*

"How long will it take to get there?" Emma asked.

"Hard to say, hard to say," the hag mumbled. "Maybe short for us, long for them. Or long for us, short for them. Moonlit paths is never the same, especially when the forest wakes."

Soon the ruined buildings of Old Downtown loomed over them. They walked past the Red Caboose, toward the spire of a cathedral. Water trickled out of a cracked fire hydrant in front of a convenience store. The store's windows were smashed and the ground was littered with candy wrappers. Strange noises broke the silence. Maybe a squirrel darting away, or a deer. Maybe not. Were there still trolls around? Cats and hag and human moved quietly in some unspoken agreement. The darkness seemed to cling to the hag, and she mumbled as they walked, counting trees and old houses, turning occasionally or doubling back.

Emma gave Jack a look as he padded beside her. He seemed tense, not quite himself—whatever that really was.

"You've been to the Deep Forest before, haven't you?" she said.

"Once, when I needed to escape," Jack said. "It's no place for a lone cat, weak and starved for magic." He shook his head. "But that was far from here, and years ago. I'd never have remembered how to get back there. All I remember is the journey home. I followed a tiny red star, and that's what brought me to Old Downtown. Convenient."

"Was it when you killed your Pride-Heart?" Emma asked.

Jack said nothing, and Emma knew she'd guessed right.

"Why'd you kill her? Why'd you become a Heart-Killer at all?"

For a while he didn't say anything, and Emma thought he wasn't going to respond. But then, very softly, he said, "Because to her I was nothing, and to me she was everything. I cared too much about her, about the magic she gave me. The magic was a leash. Or a cage. I was like those crags in the faeries' zoo. I had no choice. I needed to be free of her."

His words sent a cold shiver up Emma's spine. *So what does that make me?* she wondered. But he was the one who'd offered her the Heart's Blood to begin with. They were friends, and he couldn't use magic anymore anyway. It wasn't the same.

The hag stopped in front of an old house. Or at least, what remained of the house—a plain front door, barely hanging on by its rusted hinges, and the remnants of a moss-covered brick wall.

The hag walked up to the door, knocked on it, and then ducked through.

Emma eyed the broken wall suspiciously and went around instead. Only, when she reached the other side, the hag wasn't there.

"Not that way," came the hag's voice. "You has to go through door."

"What kind of magic is this?" Emma asked, walking back. The hag was waiting for her on the other side of the door, just as before.

"Door magic," the hag croaked. "Simplest kind. Takes you into places. Takes you out again."

"Wait!" Jack said. Emma looked behind. He seemed different somehow. Smaller. There was an unfathomable expression in his one eye. "Are you sure you want to do this? The Deep Forest is dangerous. If your sister really wants to be a faerie . . ." He sounded strange, almost unsure.

"What are you talking about?" she said. "Come on, you're the one who made this possible. You've taught me cat magic. You've made me a Pride-Heart. It's okay if you're scared. I'm scared, too, but we'll be all right."

Cricket snorted. "A Heart-Killer worried about a Pride-Heart. How ironic."

Jack glared at Cricket, then turned back to Emma. When he spoke again, he sounded like his old self. "You're right. We can't turn back now, not when we're so close. You go first."

Emma shook her head, then stepped through the door. Her cats followed. She looked around. The ruins of Old Downtown had gone. Now there were only trees. And there was a strange moonlight, more blue than any she had ever seen. It reminded her of the fake moon in the faerie nightclub on Ocean Avenue. Emma sniffed the air. It smelled like forest. Rich earth, the faint hint of some nearby animal. But there was something else — not a smell, just a feeling. Something potent and exciting and dangerous. This wasn't just the forest anymore. It was somewhere else. She could feel deep, wild magic all around her. She felt the Heart's Blood change inside her, become alive somehow. *This way*, it was saying, pulling her forward, drawing her farther into the trees.

"We walks carefully," said the hag. "This is the starts of Deep Forest. Is dangerous, tonight most dangerous. High Spring. Time for things to change and grow. Many creatures abroad worse than hags, and without love of cats or humans." The hag grinned, her mouth like a dark pit in the strange moonlight.

"We don't have time to walk carefully," Emma said. "We have to hurry."

"Humans is always hurrying," the hag grumbled. "Even when they is cats, dragging poor old hags into the dark places. But little cats must take care or they never comes out again."

# CHAPTER 19

Lights gleamed in the darkness as they made their way into the Deep Forest. Some flickered like distant bonfires, others glowed steadily like streetlights.

"What are they?" Emma asked the hag.

But it was Jack who answered. "Wisps. They lead you off your path until you're lost, then they vanish. It's easy to get lost here."

Emma didn't doubt that for a moment. Though the moonlight was unnaturally bright, a thick fog seemed to lie between the looming trees, and beyond them was only a hazy, impenetrable blackness.

There was a tension in the air, like the Deep Forest was waiting for something. Somewhere far away a horn blew, and there was the distant sound of hooves thumping on the ground. A wolf howled, and others picked up the sound. Was that what the hag meant by howlers? Branches seemed to appear suddenly out of the darkness, scratching at Emma's arms and face, pulling at her hair. She knocked one of the branches away, and there was a flutter of leathery wings. Then they were gone.

She paused. She smelled something different. Musk and damp fur. The hag seemed to sense it, too, for she stopped abruptly and sniffed.

"What is that?" Emma whispered.

"Howlers," the hag said, and she shrank back into the forest shadows.

A pair of red eyes appeared among the trees. It was almost impossible not to stare at them. Then Emma heard a growl. The sound reverberated in her chest and made the hairs on the back of her neck stand on end. Her pride hissed and pulled magic from her, and their hissing turned into roaring as they became large cats.

More red eyes appeared, drawing closer, and Emma could make out the howlers now: saber-toothed wolves, as big as any of the huge cats behind her. Emma's heart pounded as she scanned the trees, trying to figure out some clever magic that might prevent a bloody fight.

Then one of the wolves stood up on two legs. Reaching up with its paws—no, they were hands—it grabbed the fur of its head and pulled. The wolf's neck split apart, and a man's head came free. Yet even as it hung there the wolf-head still breathed, the red eyes staring at her.

Emma gasped and stumbled backward. The big cats around her growled, but she felt their fear. The hag was nowhere to be seen.

The man's head was bald, his face hairless and lined. When he opened his mouth and spoke, it was a harsh, snarling language Emma had never heard before. The sound echoed strangely among the trees, changing, then turning into words she understood.

"What sort of cat wears a human skin and travels with shadows?" the echoes said.

"I'm Emma," she said, and her voice, too, echoed among the trees. "I'm a girl and a Pride-Heart. We just want to pass."

"This is our hunting ground," the man said, and as he moved his mouth, the wolf's mouth moved as well. "Cats are not welcome here."

A few of her cats spat at this, but Emma held up a hand to calm them. She made sure her claws were retracted. "Then let us through. You won't see us again. I'm only here at all because the faeries stole my sister. They stole someone from you, too, I think. I saw a wolf in their zoo, in a glass cage."

The man and the wolf-head stared at her; the man nodded.

"It is so. But she roamed far outside our lands. No faerie would trespass among our trees to steal from us."

"I'm not here to steal, either," Emma said.

He sniffed the air and leaned forward. "You're lucky. Today is High Spring, Ostara, the end of a long sleep. A day of hunger and of hunting. To kill a human Pride-Heart would attract attention from beasts more dangerous than us. The forest has woken, as it does on this day every year, and you would be wise to stick to the path." The wolf-skin's lips pulled back in a snarl. "My pack will not trouble you, but other creatures may decide differently. Do not hunt in the moonlight. Do not kill among the trees. You have been warned."

He pulled the wolf-skin back over his head, and then only a large, red-eyed wolf remained where the man had been. It dropped back on all fours, watching her a moment longer, then turned away and disappeared into the trees, the rest of the pack following.

Emma stood still for what seemed like a long time, trembling. Even her cats, for all their strength, had gathered close. They began to shrink to their normal sizes once more.

"What did he mean about the Deep Forest being awake tonight?" Emma asked.

The air seemed to swallow her words, and the trees rustled and creaked even though there was no wind.

"Tonight the Deep Forest is alive, hungry," whispered Fat

Leon. "Hungrier than usual for High Spring, I think. Can't you feel it in the air?"

"If the faeries are using the forest's High Spring magic to change your sister, we can't have much time left," Jack said.

A shadow emerged, became solid. The hag was still there. "Faeries not far," she sang. "Listen."

Emma concentrated. Perhaps she could hear something in the distance. Wind chimes. Bells. Faerie voices. There was a brightness up ahead, an even stronger blue moonlight. They walked toward the light only to find the way blocked by trees. Low-hanging branches intertwined as if they had always been that way, though the path had seemed clear before. The spaces between the tree trunks were choked with hanging vines and thick, thorn-covered rose bushes.

"Faeries only wants invited humans," the hag said.

"We can squeeze through," Jack said. "Just try harder."

Emma pushed at the vines and tried to crawl through the bushes. Her pride followed. But it was no use. The thorns scratched her. Brambles stuck to her clothes and tangled in her hair. And everything seemed to be positioned in just the right way to snag at her feet or scratch her face. She could hear her cats yowling in pain.

Above her the rustling of the trees seemed to become a whisper. *You're not welcome here. You shouldn't be here. You want to go back. You want to run away.* Was this the faeries' way of keeping her out?

A part of her would have been glad to do exactly what the whispers said. When she turned to look back, the trees were spaced far apart, giving her plenty of room to walk through them.

"I'm not leaving without my sister," she hissed, cutting at the vines and brambles with her claws.

*She could leave,* the trees whispered, *but she wants to stay. They all want to stay.*

"She'll come with me. I know she will!" Emma said. This wasn't going to be like Nissa's eye-puppet Jen. This was Helena. Once Helena realized what was happening, what the faeries were going to do to her, she'd want to go home. Pieces of vine and branch and rosebush fell away from her claws.

*We will not let you take her. Only those that want to leave can pass.*

"Fine," Emma spat, and then, with a last effort, she managed to climb through the tangle, stumbling onto clear forest floor. The hag was already waiting for her, shadowy and insubstantial. The pride hissed and spat as they finished clawing their way through to stand beside her.

"Easy," Jack said, licking at a scratch on his side.

"Yeah, right," Emma said. "Easy."

"Shut up," Cricket hissed. "There's someone coming."

Emma ducked down behind a tree and sniffed the air. There was a sharp chemical scent that wasn't at all like the forest. Definitely something human. Shampoo or deodorant.

"I heard voices," came a boy's voice. "Should we go back and tell them someone's out here?"

A girl answered. "Doesn't matter what you hear. Corbin thinks someone's trying to sneak in, and he wants to see who. That means we have to see it or we'll be no good to the lords and ladies. Without our eyes they won't know what's going on."

"Well, hurry up, I don't want to miss the ceremony! Who knows when they'll let us up on the twenty-seventh floor again?"

"I'm going as fast as I can. You think it's easy walking on soft ground wearing heels?"

They were crashing through the forest, loud and obvious and definitely human.

Emma found Fat Leon crouching nearby and put a finger to her mouth for silence. He tilted his head at her slightly, as if to say, *You're telling us?* Emma waited until she was sure the boy and girl had passed, then she inched carefully around the tree.

She could see now that the trees ended abruptly ahead of them and that beyond them was a clearing, bright with that unnatural moonlight. Tall LED lamps slowly changed from yellow and red to white to green, casting the nearby leaves first in autumn colors, then winter, then spring and summer. A faerie in designer sunglasses sat at a foldout table at the edge of the clearing, fiddling with a laptop computer. Soft, mystical music—bells and wind chimes and flutes—flowed from huge speakers positioned around the clearing. A portable generator hummed nearby, cables spewing out of it and snaking through the grass, powering the lights and speakers.

At the far end of the clearing a spotlit wooden stage had been erected next to an impossibly tall tree that reached up into the sky until it seemed as though it would touch the stars themselves. In front of the stage were the faeries Emma had seen in the nightclub—the honeysuckle and spiderweb faeries—and more, although she didn't see Nissa. They were surrounded by a crowd of young people in elaborate outfits, watching both the stage and the faeries, and chattering excitedly.

An enormous screen was suspended from one of the tree's branches, showing a live shot of an empty stage. Only the stage wasn't empty. A shiver ran up Emma's spine as she saw the faerie standing center stage. It was the toadlike one who'd been with Helena at the nightclub. Corbin. His glamour was tall and broad-shouldered, his skin a warm olive brown, and his hair a wavy, sun-bleached chestnut shade. His brown eyes were bright and deep. The kind of eyes Helena's magazines would have called "intense."

He was holding a microphone, and a deep, smooth voice poured out of the speakers over the music.

"Welcome, friends and guests and worshippers! I hope you've all enjoyed yourselves so far, but now the real celebration begins. Tonight is a special night, my friends. Ostara. The Deep Forest is awake, and there is power in the earth and in the trees."

A hush fell over the audience as the faerie talked. It was as if he was lulling them, hypnotizing them almost. Even Emma had to shake her head to keep from nodding along excitedly. "Is Helena here?" she whispered to the hag.

The hag sniffed the air. "Close, now, and coming closer. I smell her. Afraid and excited both. Runaways smells like that, too, when they're still fresh. Best to finds them quick before there's only fear left to taste."

Corbin was still talking. "It's been a year since our last celebration, but there is only one night when we can borrow the Deep Forest's magic and perform our miracle. The transformation of humans into faeries. Only tonight. And only four chosen."

The captive audience breathed an exultant sigh, and then began to clap and cheer. A few of them were wiping away tears.

Then there came a loud *ding!* Emma glanced to her right and saw an elevator rising up out of the ground, the same one she had taken to the roof of the faerie nightclub. The doors slid open.

"And here they are now! Welcome to the Twenty-Seventh Floor!" Corbin called out.

Everyone turned to look as the four teens filed out of the elevator, led by Nissa and her eye-puppet Jen. At the front of the line was Helena, wearing the same blue-and-red dress she'd worn at the club. And she was smiling.

CRAG FACT OF THE DAY:

*"Ratters have a knack for finding out things that are*
*supposed to be secret, and have been known to work*
*as journalists and detectives as well as spies."*
CragWiki.org

# CHAPTER 20

The hag sniffed the air once more and nodded. "I've done as I promised. Good luck, little cat."

"Wait, can't you just—"

But the hag slid away into the forest, muttering to herself as she disappeared into the dark. Emma turned back to the stage.

"Have no fear, future brothers and sisters," the faerie Corbin was saying. "Come forward to embrace the forest."

Helena and the three other teenagers walked past the audience and climbed up onto the stage. Corbin took Helena's hand and

224

smiled. The music changed from bells and flutes to a low drum and a singer, crying out in a language Emma didn't recognize.

"What do we do?" she said.

"Just get out there," Jack replied. "That'll get their attention quick enough."

Emma looked nervously at all the faeries and humans. "What if he runs off with her again? Farther into the forest?"

"Then we'll track her down," Cricket said.

"You're wasting time!" Jack spat. His eye was brighter than ever in the moonlight, and he was fidgeting with some emotion Emma couldn't quite read.

"Place your hands on the sacred tree," murmured Corbin, "and become that which you desire most."

Emma could see now that the impossibly tall tree next to the stage was carved all over with runes and pictures that seemed to flow into one another. There were satyrs dancing, cats rearing up with claws extended, chains of ratters tail-to-tail, lone trolls and packs of wolves and snake people. There were creatures Emma had only read about on CragWiki and creatures she'd never heard of before. There were moons in different phases, and constellations she didn't know.

The tree had no leaves, but all manner of things hung off its branches—or were part of its branches: Emma couldn't tell. There were many-colored lanterns, glass jars with fireflies, cages made of bone that were filled with crows and bats and brightly feathered small birds that Emma had never seen before.

"What do you want us to do?" Cricket said, tense with excitement.

Emma thought. "The faeries need their humans to see. Knock the humans to the ground, stand on them, scare them so they run away or shut their eyes. But don't hurt them! Not if you don't have to. Just keep their eyes on you and away from me. Got it? Okay, everyone. On my count of three we charge. One . . ."

Helena and the three teens gathered around the tree, and placed their hands on the trunk. The carved images began to move. The crows in their cages cawed excitedly. Lanterns glowed with blue flame.

"Two . . ."

Emma stared, wide-eyed, as vines began to grow from the tree, snaking down over the four humans, wrapping around them, lifting them off the ground and binding them to the trunk, in green cocoons.

"Three!"

She didn't wait for her cats to respond. She was their Pride-Heart, and this was her hunt. She ran. She could feel them drawing magic from her, changing shape. Behind her the air filled with roars, and the humans all turned to look. They screamed and stumbled to their feet, unable to take their eyes off the cats.

"Stop them!" the faerie Corbin cried out. "It's the human Pride-Heart, she wants to ruin us!"

"But don't harm her!" Nissa shouted. "No one is to harm her!"

These contradictory instructions only served to confuse everything more. A few brave humans leaped at the cats, but they were quickly swatted aside by massive paws. A few more thought Emma would be easier prey, but her claws soon proved them wrong. As for the rest . . . a faerie enchantment could make them adore the faeries, but it couldn't make them brave, not with a pride of huge cats bearing down on them. They ran.

"Idiots! Don't take your eyes off her!" Corbin yelled, his head swiveling from side to side. "Find the girl, the little human girl, we need to see her!"

All this Emma took in with one quick glance, and then she was running past the faeries as they flailed blindly near the stage, up the steps, and past Corbin. Her claws were already out when she reached Helena.

"I knew you couldn't stay away, cat-girl!" Nissa called out. "I can hear you. Have you come to stay with Nissa at last?"

Emma ignored her. Up close, she could see the vines had thorns. But where they pierced Helena's skin only drops of clear, bright dew oozed out. Her sister's eyes were tightly closed, as if she were in a deep dream.

"Helena, it's me!" she cried. "I'm going to save you." Jack and the Toe-Chewer were beside her. "Help me get her out of this," Emma ordered, and together they scratched at the vines. But their claws just seemed to pass right through them.

"They're not real!" Emma shouted. She tried to pull Helena free, but her sister wouldn't budge.

"Well? Think of something!" Jack spat, as if it was his sister being turned into a faerie and not hers.

"Maybe I could turn into a troll for real this time and knock the tree down," the Toe-Chewer babbled. "Or you could turn me into one of those things humans use to cut down trees. A knife, right? Or you could turn her into something really little, like a fly, and then she'd be able to get out—"

*The vines are just like the faeries*, Emma thought. *Real, but not real. Nothing that cat magic couldn't deal with.*

As she focused on the vines, they became solid under her fingertips. Carefully, she began to cut them away.

"Yes!" Jack hissed. "That's it!"

Helena's eyes were wide now, and Emma could hear her trying to speak. She slashed at the vines as quickly as she dared, more worried about saving Helena's life than giving her a few scratches here and there. Dew spattered over Emma's palms where her claws bit into Helena's skin, cool and sparkling like early morning moonlight.

As soon as Helena's mouth was free of vines she started shouting. "Emma, stop, you're ruining everything!"

"It's all right," Emma said, still slicing through the vines. "You think you love him, but you don't. You don't know what you're saying."

Emma heard her cats fighting, felt them using her magic. A mountain lion blurred past her as Cricket leaped toward a human that had pulled out his cell phone and was desperately jabbing at the screen, trying to dial. She knocked him to the ground and smacked the phone out of his hands, sending it sliding across the grass.

"Stop it, Emma, please! You don't understand, you don't know what this means to me!"

Emma freed Helena's hands, only to have to fend off Helena's attempts to push her away. She clawed through the remaining vines gripping Helena's legs, then retracted her claws and took her sister by the hand, pulling her away from the tree. "Come on, I'm getting you out of here before they turn you into one them."

"Emma, you're not listening to me!"

It was true, Emma hadn't been listening, or paying much attention. She barely saw Helena's hand rise. *Crack!*

Emma sat back on the stage, stunned. Her head swam. Helena had slapped her. Hard. Emma shook her head, trying to clear it—just in time to see Helena running from her, straight into Corbin's arms.

"Corbin! Corbin, I'm here, I'm sorry," Helena cried. "I didn't know about her, I swear! Please don't make me leave. I want to be like you, I want to be with you!"

"It's all right," Corbin said softly as he stroked her hair. "I found out she was your sister. One of her cats told me. I knew she would try to find you. I just hoped it wouldn't be tonight."

"Why didn't you tell me our Lady Helena had such an interesting family?" Nissa said. "Oh, the cat-girl has to stay. Why don't you trade Helena for her? You can get another Helena, they're all over the place."

"Shut up, Nissa," Corbin growled.

Elsewhere in the clearing, the cats had done as Emma ordered. Too scared to run off into the darkness beyond the trees, the humans huddled together in small groups while cats circled around them, growling and snapping their teeth and occasionally administering a scratch if they caught a human so much as looking at the stage. Nearby, the faeries stood, blind and furious and powerless.

Powerless except for their hold over Helena.

"What are you doing?" Jack said to Emma. "Get up! Stop sitting there trembling like a little mouse!"

"She hit me," Emma said, touching her face. It didn't even hurt that much, except . . . except Helena had actually hit her.

"So? The last girl you tried to save threw you off a roof."

"I know, but . . . she's my sister. I'm here to rescue her!"

230

Jack rubbed his head against her arm. He purred. "You won't rescue her by sitting there. You have to be smart and sneaky, remember? Like me." He jumped up on her shoulder. "Now get up."

Emma got up.

"Emma! Call off your cats, Emma!" Helena said, clinging to Corbin's arm. "Please. Can't you see you're spoiling everything?"

"If you don't call off your cats," the honeysuckle faerie said, "Corbin will have to ask Helena to run off into the forest, or maybe hang herself from the sacred tree. You wouldn't want that, would you?"

"No!" Emma and Corbin yelled at the same time.

For a moment the clearing was silent except for the growl of massive cats and the whimper of humans.

"I don't think you should do that," Jack said, loud enough for everyone to hear.

"What is this?" Corbin said. "Who are you?"

"What are you doing?" Emma hissed.

"Trust me. I have a plan," Jack said into her ear. "Well, I had a plan. It's been changing as we go. You need to turn Helena into one of us. Into a cat."

"What? Why—?"

Jack's claws dug into her shoulder. "Trust me."

"What are you even doing here, Emma?" Helena said.

"I'm trying to rescue you!"

Helena took a step toward her. "But Emma, I don't want to be rescued. I never did. I want to be here. I'm *happy* here. Can't you understand that? Mom and Dad were driving me crazy. I was going to move out in a year or two anyway. Does it really matter when I leave?"

"What about me?" Emma said quietly. "Was I horrible, too?"

"No! No, of course not. I just—" She looked away, and Emma noticed Corbin didn't reprimand her, even though he had to be using her eyes to see Emma. "I meant to call you, or send you an e-mail. But it's easy to forget things with the faeries. Sometimes a single day can take forever."

"That's just an excuse," Emma said. "If you knew you were forgetting, you could have done something. I missed you. You have no idea what's been going on. You don't even care."

"Of course I care," Helena said.

"Nissa cares," said Nissa. "Nissa wouldn't abandon you."

"If you really care, then you'll come home," Emma said, ignoring the willow-leaf faerie again.

"Emma, that's not fair," Helena said. "I'm allowed to be happy, too."

"Well what about Mom and Dad? They gave up everything trying to find you."

"It's not that simple."

"If you could just see what he really looks like, though! He's not human. He's like . . . he's some kind of toad thing! How can you love that?"

"Get on with it!" Jack hissed.

"I'm sorry, Emma," Helena said.

But she wasn't really sorry. She wanted to stay, and she didn't seem to care about anything or anyone else. Well, except for her toad faerie. This wasn't the Helena Emma knew. The faeries must have done something to her, cast a spell that didn't just change what Helena could see, but what she believed. Helena would want to come home, to be with her family again. Emma had to believe that.

She rushed forward and wrapped Helena in a hug, pressing her face against her sister's shoulder. "I'm not leaving you here. I'm not."

Helena tried to pull away. Emma extended her claws, keeping her close.

"Emma, ow! What are you doing?"

She focused her magic, ready to fight against someone who didn't want to change, and Helena's cry turned into a yowl as she shrank and became a tiny brown cat even smaller than the Toe-Chewer.

"Well, that's an interesting new way to make more cats," Fat Leon said from somewhere.

Nissa giggled and clapped her hands, bouncing up and down like an excited child. "Someone get over here so I can see. This sounds so fabulous!"

"What did you do to her?" Corbin yelled. He tried to run at Emma, but he could only see what Helena saw.

Emma grabbed cat-Helena by the scruff of her neck, and turned her to face Corbin. The cat began to tremble.

"She can see you," Emma said.

Corbin took a hesitant step forward, watching himself—his real toad self—through Helena's cat eyes. Helena backed away, pressing herself against Emma's chest. "No. Please," Corbin whispered. "Helena, please. I love you. It won't matter once you change. You'll see the world through human eyes, you'll only see the magic. What you really look like won't matter. You won't be able to see yourself." He turned toward Emma, even though he couldn't see her. "Please. Don't do this. Change her back."

The power of his glamour, the sadness and desperation in his voice might have broken Emma's human heart. But the Pride-Heart wasn't moved at all. She shook her head. "She doesn't want to stay with you now. She doesn't want to lose her eyes and look like some kind of monster. That means I can take her home. And if any of you try to stop me, if any of you come near me or my family or any of my friends . . . I'll turn all your humans into cats. Then they will know what you are. Everyone will."

The faeries said nothing to this, but Emma could feel their anger and fear. No wonder Corbin had been afraid of a human Pride-Heart.

"Well, that's settled, then," Jack said. He sounded almost happy. "Now, you need four in the ceremony, don't you?"

"Four people," Corbin spat. "Not three people and a cat, if that's what you're suggesting."

"He's not suggesting that," Emma said, turning to Jack. "Are you?"

But Jack spoke as if she hadn't said anything. "What does the forest care what kind of thing it changes?" he purred. "Cat, human, any creature that thinks and speaks would probably do. And I'm the solution to your problem. You've returned my Pride-Heart's sister to her, so you're one short. Take me instead. Turn me into whatever I desire. Give me back my magic."

CRAG FACT OF THE DAY:
*"Do not open image texts when you don't know the sender!*
*You can catch magical diseases such as Ficklerot by*
*reading runes or hexes on your phone."*
CragWiki.org

# CHAPTER 21

"Jack . . ." Emma said. "What are you doing?"

Jack turned to her. "Haven't you been paying attention?" he said. "I'm nothing without magic. A Heart-Killer. Not even a real cat." He met her eyes. "I gave you the Heart's Blood. I helped you find your sister. Now this is what I want. What I always wanted."

"As if what you want matters, Heart-Killer," Cricket growled.

"You don't deserve magic. Even becoming a faerie is too good for you," said Fat Leon.

"So it was never about me. It was all about getting your magic back." Emma felt tears well up. Human tears. "You didn't care about me at all. You were just pretending to be my friend so you could get what you wanted." *Heart-Killer,* she thought.

"I told you caring for things was a trap," said Jack, but his voice sounded small.

"You have your sister. Take her and your cats and leave us alone," one of the humans screamed. "Leave us alone!"

"Yes, take your Helena and go," the honeysuckle faerie said. "You can't turn everyone here into cats. I can hear the exhaustion in your voice, Emma. What'll happen to you when your magic finally runs out? When your cats can't protect you anymore?"

Emma's pride hissed.

"This is getting boring," said Nissa. "If your cat wants to take his chances with the tree, he's welcome. Otherwise one of these other humans will serve well enough to keep the numbers right."

Emma gritted her teeth. "They think they love you, but they don't," she said. "How can they when they don't even know what you are?" But she knew the honeysuckle faerie was right. The Heart's Blood felt faint. The threads of magic connecting her to her cats were weakening. Some of them were struggling to hold their shape.

"As if mere sight can tell you what we are," the honeysuckle faerie laughed. "We've never turned a cat before. And such a dark heart. I wonder what kind of creature he'll become?"

"Who cares?" Nissa said.

"Jack, please," Emma said. "Don't do this."

Jack looked at the faeries, then back at Emma. His tail snapped back and forth.

"Please," Emma said, so quietly she didn't think he would even hear.

Into the silence of the clearing came an odd sound, like the jingling of a bell. It was so familiar, and so out of place, that for a moment Emma didn't recognize it. Then she did. It was a ringtone. The phone that Cricket had knocked to the ground was ringing, its screen lit up with a text message.

Then another phone rang out, and another, until a chorus of phones sounded all over the clearing. The humans glanced around nervously and fingered their pockets. Emma hesitated, then took two steps and picked up the phone. **WANT TO SEE WHAT FAERIES REALLY LOOK LIKE?** the message said, and beneath it was a video. Emma tapped it and the image of a grinning ratter popped open on the screen:

*"You think you know something about magic,"* it squeaked. *"You think you know something about faeries. But for hundreds of years they've toyed with humans, and you've loved them for it. You give them everything, and they take everything—even your children. But secrets and knowings want to be free. They want to be discovered . . ."*

Here and there the humans were sneaking glances at their phones and tapping on the screen. Soon the ratter's voice filled the clearing.

"All it takes is a little cat magic to break through the enchantment, and a lot of clever ratter tricks to get you all to see it. Want to see what becoming a faerie really means? Watch!"

Then the video jerked, and instead of the ratter's face, it showed the clearing as it had looked before Emma and her cats had stormed in: the faeries sitting in front of the stage, surrounded by their human eye-puppets; Corbin talking into his microphone. Just as Emma had seen them.

And now she understood. Just as *she* had seen them. As a Pride-Heart. Not as a human.

For a moment she was back in the ratter tunnels, her tail fused to the ratterking. She remembered the feeling that she still had a tail, even though there was nothing there, that something remained when she had sliced through it. Something *had* remained. An implant. A wire.

"We want to be there when you find your sister . . . you are part of the ratterking always."

The ratterking had wanted a spy, and not just any spy. They had known she would be able to see through the faeries' glamour before she knew it herself. And now they were using that ratter-tail implant to look at the faeries through her cat eyes, recording what she saw and beaming it out to the whole world.

Faeries without their glamour. It was the ultimate secret, and now it was out in the open.

The faeries screamed. Humans began to shout and cry out.

The video ended with the text **Pass this link to 10 people and have a magical year!** followed by a link to a CragWiki article on faeries, hacked to include a link to the same video Emma had just seen.

"Do you even realize what you've done?" Corbin cried, his head swiveling as he tried to find Emma. "The humans will come after us, and their own children will try to protect us."

"Let them all go, then," Emma said. "Let them go and leave the city forever."

"Liars! Faeries are all liars!" someone shouted.

And then all the humans started to run every which way.

"Leave them!" Emma shouted to her cats. "Help me free the others from the tree!"

Out of the corner of her eye she saw Jack racing toward the sacred tree, followed by the rest of her pride. The wooden stage buckled and creaked as they all leaped up onto it. Jack stood between her and the cocooned teens, next to the vines that had held Helena so tightly. As tightly as Emma held her sister now, clutching her to her chest with one arm. But her other arm was free.

Emma flicked out her claws. So did Jack. For a moment each stared at the other.

"You can't fight me," Emma said.

"I've killed a Pride-Heart before over magic," he spat. "Try me, or stay out of my way!" He backed up toward the tree. The vines hissed and slithered, reaching for him greedily, hungrily. As if the ritual wanted to complete itself.

Above their heads, the television that had been showing the stage flickered, and suddenly it, too, was running the ratter's face while his voice squeaked from the speakers: *"You think you know something about magic!"*

"We'll find some other way to get you magic, there has to be something else out there," Emma said. "But not this. Please. Magic isn't what's important."

*Please don't leave me.*

"What do you know about it?" Jack whispered. "You still think like a human. You don't understand what it's like for me."

"I can't let them turn these kids into faeries. They have brothers and sisters, too. Parents. People who love them and don't know where they are. Jack, please. Don't ask me to pick between helping you and helping them."

His eye met hers, and he seemed to look into her. Just then one of the vines snaked out and wrapped itself around his leg. He spat in annoyance and jumped back, clawing the vine away. Then he stopped suddenly. There was surprise in his eyes. Shock.

For just a moment, without realizing it, he'd chosen her over his magic.

It was enough for Emma.

She leaped forward, slashing at the vines that held the other teens. The tree's branches rattled angrily and the vines struggled, but they were no match for Emma's claws. Her pride surrounded Jack, hissing and spitting in case he tried to hurt her or stop her, but he only stood and watched, wide-eyed.

The teenagers in the vines struggled, crying in despair at being freed. All of them seemed part-faerie already, their flesh shimmering strangely, and one of them had turned green, his skin as silky as a flower petal. But they all still had their eyes. She expected tears, attacks, but they seemed disoriented — frightened, even. They staggered away, following the crowds.

Emma hugged the little brown cat that was Helena. "We need to get out of here," she said to her pride, then turned to Jack. "Thank you."

He shook himself. Then he spat at her and leaped to the tree, scratching at it desperately. But the vines hung, slashed and lifeless. The ceremony had needed four. He'd missed his chance.

"I don't know why I hesitated," he said. He seemed confused.

"Because you're my friend. And you do care. You cared about those kids."

Jack stopped and looked at her. "No. I didn't care about them. And I wasn't supposed to care about you, either. Don't you get it? I didn't do any of this for you. I brought you the Heart's Blood because I knew you'd try to help your sister. And by trying to get her back, by taking on the faeries, you'd help me get my magic

242

back. And I was right! It was an insane plan, and it worked! But I let myself become your pet, as if you really were my Pride-Heart. I let you put a leash around me even without magic. Now what good am I? Sooner or later you'll get tired of having me around, and then what?"

"That's not true!" Emma cried, reeling from everything Jack was saying to her.

"What happens when your parents decide they're tired of the trailer park? I won't be able to go with you then. Maybe the others won't mind if you turn them into mice and hide them in little cages, but a cat without magic will just make things harder for you."

"We'll think of something!" Emma said. "I won't let my mom kick you out. You're still my friend."

"I don't need friends!" Jack hissed. "I don't need a Pride-Heart! I don't need a pride! I don't need anyone. I don't need *you*."

Then he turned away from her and ran.

"Jack!" she yelled.

He stopped. He looked back, his eye flashing yellow in the darkness.

Her voice caught. Whatever she had meant to say was gone. "Even if you didn't mean to be, you were still my friend. Weren't you? That's why you didn't let the tree take you, wasn't it?"

"I don't know," he said. "I don't know."

Then he was gone. Emma called after him again, but it was no use. She had to let him go. And she had to find her way home, which, thanks to Jack, she knew how to do.

She gathered her pride around her and held Helena-the-cat close. Then, looking up, she found the tiny red star above the trees and began to walk.

"Cat-girl Emma!" echoed Nissa's voice behind her. "I know your name! I'll find you again one day!"

*"The discovery of a crag plot to turn human teens into faeries has led to a nationwide increase in anti-crag and anti-magic feeling. Some government officials have even called for a ban on all media showing faeries in a positive light."*

CragWiki.org

# CHAPTER 22

Two weeks later, Emma stood at the edge of the forest, the Toe-Chewer at her side. Watching. Waiting. There had been no sign of Jack. Now that she was back, what had happened in the Deep Forest almost didn't feel real. Like it hadn't really happened. But sometimes she thought she could feel the sting of Helena's slap on her cheek, and her chest still ached from the things Jack had said.

Jack's red star had led them home, just as he said it would. She'd turned Helena back to herself on the metal steps of the trailer and her sister had crumpled there, her hands over her face, sobbing. Then her parents had come running out of the trailer, falling to their knees beside Helena. Emma thought there would probably be a lot more crying to come. And a lot of explanations, too. But for the time being, she was just happy to have her family back.

Her mom came up to stand behind her now. She put a hand on Emma's shoulder.

"We've been making some calls. We might be able to find a private school for you. They won't even consider you as long as we're living here, but I thought once we moved—"

Emma shook her head. "We can't move. My pride is here, and they need me."

Her mom was quiet for a while. Then she sighed and pulled Emma closer. "Emma . . . he might not come back. You know that. He was never your friend."

"He was," Emma said. "He just didn't realize it. He'll come back, I know he will. He has to." But if the things he said were true . . . No. She couldn't believe that. He was coming back.

"Your sister has something to say to you," her mom said as Helena stepped out of the trailer, and she gave Helena a pointed stare.

"Thank you for saving me," Helena said, but her voice was flat and emotionless. She'd hardly looked at Emma since she had come home.

"She just needs time," her mom murmured in Emma's ear. "I'll leave you two to talk, okay?" Then she gave them each a quick hug and went back inside.

"I'm not sorry for rescuing you," Emma said.

"You'll never understand," Helena whispered. A tear rolled down her cheek, sparkling like dew. Helena smelled different since Emma brought her home, too. She smelled like rain and earth and the Deep Forest. She looked like the same old Helena, but there was something not quite the same anymore.

"Corbin loved me, Emma. You took that away from me. I can't forgive you for that."

Emma nodded. Helena had said the same thing every day since she'd been home. Each time she sounded a little less sure of her words, but it was hard to hear her say them. It was going to take time, their parents said. But Emma had no idea how long a faerie enchantment could last once you were no longer in their presence.

The Toe-Chewer rubbed his head against Helena's shoe. "Do you have anything to eat?" he asked, looking up at her with huge eyes. "I like that chicken from a can. It's like a sparrow, but without the feathers."

Helena's face softened, just the tiniest bit, as she looked down at the little tabby. "Come inside and we'll see," she said.

Chloe flew down from her perch on a nearby tree and landed next to Emma. "She hasn't tried to escape again, has she?"

"Not since that first day," Emma said.

"So, what's it like having a sister?" Chloe asked.

Emma thought for a minute before answering. "It's a lot like having a friend that lives with you and shares all your stuff without asking. And you fight with them a lot but kind of have to love them anyway."

"That sounds awesome. Especially the fighting part. I don't get to fight very often because when I get mad I use my voice and then everyone around me gets *really* mad."

Emma smiled. "I don't think I'd like fighting with you, then."

"Oh." Chloe frowned and leaned back, staring at Emma. "Maybe I wouldn't make a good sister for a cat-girl after all."

Emma put her hand on Chloe's wing. "I don't know, but you make a pretty good friend."

"I'm sorry about Jack," Chloe said.

"Yeah," Emma said softly. "Me too."

They stood facing the forest together for a while.

"What's that?" Chloe said, ruffling her feathers.

"What's what?" But then Emma smelled him, and saw him step out from between the trees. She watched, unable to speak, as he sauntered past her pride as he always had, ignoring their low hissing.

"Jack," she finally managed to say.

He yawned. "You said you'd help me find magic. I assume you've been looking into it?"

"I . . . I didn't look," Emma said. "I didn't know if you were . . ."

"I figured you'd end up lazy without me around," Jack said. "Just like the rest of your pride. Are you going to let me in? I'm tired of sleeping on dirt. Your bed is a lot more comfortable."

Emma reached out to touch him. Jack rubbed his head against the palm of her hand and purred. "I'm glad you're back," she said. "It wasn't fair to get Helena back only to lose you." He didn't say anything, but the purring got louder. Chloe made a gagging noise, and Emma laughed. "But if you're going to sleep on my bed again, you'll need a bath."

# ACKNOWLEDGMENTS

We are grateful to our friends and family for their constant encouragement and support along the way. Special thanks to Diane Turnshek; without her, we'd never have met. Thanks to Jenn Kastroll, for being the best supporter and friend we could ever have, and for reading anything and everything we send her.

We thank Verla Kay's Blueboarders for their support and advice, as well as the Apocalypsies, for reminding us the world isn't over if we make a mistake.

A big thank-you to our wonderful editors Imogen and Rachel for their hard work and dedication, and of course to Barry and the rest of the Chicken House team.

Finally, many thanks to our amazing agent, who, if he's reading this, should flip to the front of the book.